# BLINDSIDED BY LOVE

## MONICA WALTERS

# INTRODUCTION

Hello, readers!

Thank you for purchasing and/or downloading this book. This work of art contains explicit language, lewd sex scenes, mild violence, moments of grief/depression, and topics that may be sensitive to some readers.

While this is the fourth country hood love story, it is the first of The Henderson Family Series. There are many more to come, along with a few spin-offs. The other country hood characters are mentioned but aren't important to the development of this story. However, they are important for stories to come in this series. Here's the list.

*8 Seconds to Love*
*Breaking Barriers to Your Heart*
*Training My Heart to Love You*

Also, please remember that your reality isn't everyone's reality. What may seem unrealistic or unrelatable to you could be very real and relatable to someone else. But also keep in mind that despite the previous statement, this is a fictional story.

This is the first of the Henderson Family country hood love stories! Get acclimated with country living and rodeo life from a black man's perspective. Enjoy Storm and Aspen's journey to love!

Monica

# CHAPTER 1

## ASPEN

*This nigga gets on my muthafucking nerves.*

That was what I thought every time Carlos asked me to do something for him. According to him, he worked all day, and he needed his woman to be his peace. *Fuck his peace.* Now, if only I could get my mouth to say just a portion of what my mind thought, I would be doing good. We'd been together for three years, and we moved in with one another a year ago. Carlos was everything my parents wanted for me. He came from money and was an investment banker, making a pretty decent living for himself.

His family had prestige like mine, and they couldn't wait until our families would be joined together through our holy matrimony. Carlos was a gorgeous man, but he was extremely chauvinistic. He didn't want me to work, because as his woman, I belonged in the house, cooking his meals and having his babies. He could kiss my big, black ass. I told him from the very beginning that I wouldn't stop working. That was one thing I couldn't bend on. There was no way I would completely lose myself being with him. As a free-lance journalist, I was able to work when I wanted to, but I found myself writing and researching all the time, which seemed to unnerve him. It had gotten to the point where I didn't like being around him all the time and that was the easiest excuse to use to get away.

There was a story I'd been watching in Nome, Texas, and Monday morning, which was in two days, I would be taking a trip there whether he liked it or not. It was a small town about two hours away from where I lived in Katy, Texas. The ranchers there had something suspicious going on with their livestock. They were dropping like flies. Everything from goats to hogs to cattle were mysteriously dying. No one outside of the community seemed to care about it, so they were getting very little exposure. I planned to change that.

After putting Carlos's plate in the dishwasher, I poured him the glass of wine he asked for. "Thanks, Pen. Could you hand me the remote?"

*I hate when he calls me Pen.* He thought it was cool since I was a writer. I cut my eyes at him but grabbed the remote from the coffee table while he watched from his recliner. *Lazy ass.* One good day, my thoughts were going to spill from my lips and shock the fuck out of his ass. With him, I was proper and pristine, carrying myself like the stereotypical lady; not cursing, not being loud in public, being polite, and catering to my man. My parents had even invested in sending me to a charm school of sorts when I was a kid.

The only sport I was allowed to play was tennis. My heart yearned for volleyball, just so the guys could see these thick ass legs and ass in those tight shorts. However, the tennis skirt was good enough for that job until I realized not many of the black guys frequented the matches. The preppy ass white guys turned their nose up at all this melanin in a short, white skirt.

They wouldn't have been able to handle me anyway. I was a thick ass, black queen that would rock their entire world. It wasn't until graduate school that someone appreciated all this drip my size twenty frame could offer. They had to get past my mind first before they could experience that pleasure-filled ride. I had to let them know that just because I was a big girl didn't mean I wasn't agile, flexible, and deadly when it came to inflicting pleasure.

I went to my room and started getting my things packed while he was watching TV. I'd break the news to him later today or tomorrow. I just didn't feel like arguing with him. Whenever I needed to do something for me, he always took that as me not having time for him. *Like, nigga, get'cho life!* I was reaching my breaking point with him, but my family had put me in a difficult predicament. When I'd told my mama of the difficulties I was having with him, she took his damn side. She'd asked, *"What woman doesn't want a man like that? He wants to take care of you. Let him."*

Just thinking about her response had me rolling my eyes. She wouldn't understand that I'd fallen out of love with Carlos. The minute I'd decided to move in with him, things had changed. Where he had been supportive of my career before, he'd done a total one-eighty. Whoever came up with the statement that you didn't truly know a person until you lived with them, ain't never lied. He was practically everything I thought I wanted. Carlos was fine as hell; the color of almonds with soft, thick lips. He wore his hair in a tapered fade and had a beard.

What took the cake was the way he looked at me when we first met at a gala put on by Hermann Memorial Hospital. I'd always been a big girl and was confident in how beautiful I was, but baby, he gave me a new attitude. This six-feet-three-inch nigga was cut just enough for me. He was romantic, affectionate, and crazy about me.

We'd seen half the world together and had planned on seeing the rest together as well. We'd taken trips to Paris, the Bahamas, Rio, and Australia. Our hopes were to go to South Africa, Jamaica, and Belize. However, if shit didn't change around here, he would be visiting those places without me.

After getting my suitcase packed, I could hear my phone ringing in the front room where I'd left it when I poured his wine.

It stopped ringing, so either they'd hung up or he'd…. "Pen! Your mom is on the phone."

*I hate when he answers my got damn phone.* I stomped out of the room to the front room where he was still in his recliner, about to yell my name again. He stretched his arm out to me as I took the phone from him. "Hello?"

"Hello, Aspen. How are you?"

"Hello, Mom. I'm great. How about you?"

"Marvelous. I wanted to remind you of the gala that your dad and I are spearheading this year to raise money for Alzheimer research. I would really like you to be there to do the writeup on it."

"Okay. Will Dallas be there?"

Dallas was my brother. My mama had named us after cities she'd spent an enormous amount of time in. Aspen, Colorado and Dallas, Texas. "Yes. He agreed to take the photographs."

"Okay. When is it?"

"It's not for two months, but you know I like to be prepared."

"Yes, ma'am. I'm putting it on my calendar now."

"Thanks so much, Aspen. How are things between you and Carlos?"

"Never better," I responded unenthusiastically.

She never noticed the change in my tone. If she did, she always ignored it. "Okay, baby. Well, I have to go. We ought to meet for brunch tomorrow."

"Ruggles?"

"Sounds great, baby. See you at ten."

Ruggles was the only place we went for brunch. So, it wasn't hard to guess. As soon as I ended the call, I turned around to see Carlos wasn't in his recliner. *Shit!* I hadn't hidden my suitcase yet. Just as I got to the bedroom, he was coming out with a frown on his face. "Going somewhere?"

"Yes. I have a writeup to do, and it's gonna take me a couple of days. I'll be staying in Beaumont and driving to Nome, Texas."

"So, you going to the middle of nowhere and wasn't gonna tell me anything?"

"I planned to tell you tomorrow. I just knew there was no point in telling you any sooner because you would be against it no matter when you knew about it."

"So, wait until the last minute so you didn't have to deal with me telling you that you need to stay home."

"Yes. That'll be less time we have to argue about this. It's the same sh—show every time I take a trip."

*Ladies don't use such perverse language. Watch what you allow to come out of your mouth, Aspen. No man wants a woman with a dirty mouth.*

It was what I thought about every time I almost slipped and cursed aloud. My mother used to tell me that all the time growing up, just for saying shut up. She'd once heard me telling my brother he sucked, and I could have sworn someone had died. She lost her damn mind on me. If she knew like I did, every man wanted a woman with a 'dirty' mouth. It was one of the things her precious Carlos loved about me. "You know, tons of women would love to be in your position," his bitch ass said, taking me away from my thoughts.

"You know what? If you're so unhappy with me, why don't you go find someone else since there are tons that want to be in my position? If they can take my position in your life, then they can have it."

*Stupid muthafucka.* If I wasn't going to brunch with my mama tomorrow, I'd leave tonight. Being threatened wasn't something I took lightly. Whether he wanted to accept it or not, he was the one that was privileged in this relationship. While he considered my job miniscule, I was making more than he did, unbeknownst to him or anyone else. My nest egg was humungous since he wanted to be the man and pay all the bills. I'd found an extremely nice loft that would accommodate me. I hadn't paid a deposit because I wanted to give him time to get his act together but fuck him.

"Aspen, you know I love you. I don't want anyone else. All the things you do to me mentally, physically, and emotionally are at levels unattainable for anyone else. I just wanna be your king in all aspects. What is it that I'm not doing that makes you feel like you have to be out there grinding, getting your own coin, when I got all the coins in the bag for you? Do I need to open you a separate account? I mean, what is it?"

He came closer to me and lightly slid his finger down my ear to my spot right beneath it on my neck. The art of distraction. He had that shit down to a science. Carlos knew that it was hard for me to resist him sexually. Despite his flaws, he could make my shit submit to him every time. I gently pushed him away. "Carlos, this has nothing to do with you. I love writing. It's my passion in life. It's the one thing I do that brings joy to my soul. You don't feel that satisfaction when you go to work?"

He pulled me closer to him again and stared into my eyes. I really believed that he had a fucked up sense of what love was. It wasn't totally his fault, but as a man, he should allow himself to be open to things with the woman he loved. "I feel that satisfaction when I'm with you and when I'm inside of you, Aspen."

I almost rolled my eyes. We could never have a serious conversation without him making it sexual. His hands slid to my ass, and my eyes closed involuntarily. I was a sexual being, especially once he got me started. While he was only the third guy I'd ever been with, I was experienced in every sense of the word and could work shit out without him having to do a thing but get hard. Kissing my spot, I moaned softly, and that was all the confirmation he needed. The conversation was done until I came down from orgasmic heaven.

# CHAPTER 2

## STORM

"Nigga, don't come at me like I'm just stupid, na. I told you I would help you out by fixing this piece of shit you driving, but don't think I'm gon' do the shit for free. That's why I don't deal with family."

"Storm, you think five hundred is a discount?"

"Man, what the fuck you talkin' 'bout? I replaced yo' fucking transmission. Five hundred don't even cover the cost of the transmission. Google that shit if you want to. I told you not to get this fucked up F-150 because Riley ran this shit in the ground, but you wouldn't listen."

I watched my cousin rub the top of his head like he was thinking shit over. Just because my family practically owned Nome didn't mean I was handing out freebies. I wasn't just accepting freebies, either. I worked hard for this strip of land I had on the highway, prime real estate for a small business owner. It was a full-service mechanic shop and service center. While I was a mechanic, I had other employees that fixed tires on little Mini Coopers all the way to tractor tires, changed oil, and did alignments.

I was doing well, especially to say I was in a small town. My bread and butter was working on tractors and other machinery the farmers used around here. My last name helped secure my clientele because people trusted that Henderson last name. I was the youngest of seven kids, and we all owned something. My parents owned a lot of land that they used as grass farms, hay fields, and where they kept the shitload of cattle they owned. They even had rice fields as well.

The problem with this shit was that family that didn't even try to do shit for themselves thought they were supposed to benefit from our hard work, like this nigga standing in front of me. "Storm, I have three hundred to my name."

"You knew that you couldn't afford the work I was doing, but yo' conniving ass let me do all that work, and you bring a funky three hundred dollars for a job that should have cost you at least three grand? You on my shit list, for real."

"You don't want the three hundred?"

"Oh, you gon' give me that shit." I snatched it out his hand. "If I wanted to, I could put a mechanic lean on yo' shit. This yo' last freebie. Take this shit off my property before I fuck you up, Dre."

I didn't know why he wanted to test me. There was a reason everybody called me by my middle name instead of Seven. I guess my mama ran out of names, and since I was baby number seven, that's what the fuck she named me. Seven Storm Henderson. They called me Storm because I had a temper and it could come out of nowhere. When it did, all of Nome had better watch out, 'cause I rained on everybody's fucking parade.

I didn't normally take no shit like Dre pulled today without fucking a nigga up. My heart was good as gold, but no nigga was finna get over on me. Dre knew better. I went to get his keys and stopped at his truck. Looking back at him to see him on the phone, I slid under that shit and cracked his oil pan with a wrench. *Ignant muthafucka.* He could play if he wanted to, but he was gon' suffer some consequences with my ass.

I slid from under it and lowered the jack, then drove the truck out to him. Leaving a copy of the invoice on his seat, I threw the

8

keys at him. He barely dodged that shit, too. "Storm! I'm sorry, dude."

"Get the fuck outta here before I change my mind about letting you leave."

He got his ass in that truck and peeled out. I wanted to take that wrench and fuck him up. Throwing my towel after wiping my face, I went inside the bay area and cleaned up a bit, preparing to shut down shop. He was gon' know some shit was wrong when he had oil leaking everywhere. *Punk ass nigga.* My mama's people were the worst when it came to shit like this. Always thought somebody had to do shit for them, and they weren't doing shit for themselves.

I gathered all my uniforms, rags, and towels to bring to the washateria one of my sisters owned. Once I loaded them on the back of my truck, I locked the shop up. Saturdays were always the busiest days. I worked more in those five hours than I did almost all week. I had another mechanic that usually worked with me during the week, but he did most of the work. I gave him off every other Saturday, though. Dre better be glad, too, because I wouldn't have shown him my somewhat lenient side in front of him. He would have gotten fucked up.

Going down the road to Tiffany's Washateria, I gave a head nod to the people waving at me passing by. What I loved about Nome was that it was a close-knit community where everybody looked out for each other. Only about six hundred people in its population, I rarely heard of violent acts occurring. There was the local drug dealer, but I never really heard of many issues from him. He was just as involved in the community as everybody else, and everybody knew what he did.

When I got to Tiffany's, I unloaded my laundry, then went inside. "What's up, y'all," I said to the patrons that had all said hello.

When I got to the counter, ignant ass Cici was at the register. "Heeeey, Storm. How you doin', baby?"

"I'm good. You a'ight?" I asked, waiting on her to say something crazy.

"Naw. This lil nigga I wanna hook up with act like he ain't got time for a real woman. I mean, I know I'm old enough to be his mama and shit, but that don't mean a damn thing. I'll put it on him so good he'll be sucking his damn thumb afterwards."

I laughed and shook my head. It was the same shit every time I came in here. "Who you talkin' 'bout, Cici?"

"Aww fuck, Storm. You know I'm talkin' 'bout the nigga that can come through here like a tornado, hurricane, or tsunami. You in here acting all friendly and shit today."

"Ain't nothing about me friendly."

"Well, shit. Unleash that storm on my ass."

I couldn't help but laugh as Tiffany came from the back and rolled her eyes. "I knew it had to be you in here disrupting the ambiance."

"Tiff, no offense, but this is a washateria. Somebody need to disrupt the hot, tired ass mood in this bitch."

Cici had no tact, not an ounce of professionalism in her body. But everybody knew her and expected that shit out of her. She really was the same age with my mama, and they'd known each other since grade school. But like a lot of people around here, they just couldn't escape poverty. I chuckled at Tiffany's facial expression, then engaged Cici. "So, what'chu gon' do with all this man, Cici. I'm six-foot-eight, baby."

"Shit, give me a shot and you'll see."

"Cici! Storm is only twenty-eight. You have a son close to his age!"

"And? That don't stop shit."

Cici couldn't contain her laughter any longer. It didn't matter how much we clowned, Tiffany always got bent out of shape. I kissed Cici on the cheek, then Tiffany as I left my shit there for them to take care of. They handled my laundry once a week, and I appreciated it. When I left, I went home to shower.

People that didn't know who I was took me as a thug ass nigga. I had a somewhat thuggish demeanor that my dad didn't too much care for, which included tatts and a snatch out platinum grill. I rarely wore the grill these days, though. Regardless of all that, I owned a five-bedroom house in the woods, practically. I built it next to one of my dad's hay fields. I didn't advertise who I was to some of the older people. Since I was the youngest, a lot of people had lost track.

Tiffany was right above me at thirty-one years old. My oldest brother was forty-three, and everybody knew his ass and exactly who he was. He owned a tractor business, so he interacted with a lot of the old money in Nome. I interacted with a few that brought their equipment to me, but not many. I was rarely on the service side of my business and that was what most of them brought their equipment in for; tires or oil changes. My other two sisters had opened a catering service, one of my brothers owned a barbershop, and the other partnered with a friend to open a convenience store.

So, it was true that we had Nome sewed up. The liquor store was owned by someone else, but she was aging and would be looking to sell her business soon. Jasper, my brother that was the barber, was already in talks with her about purchasing it from her. He and I were the closest. We had a lot in common, and he had a temper somewhat like mine, but his only emerged when he was provoked. I had to see him in a little bit for him to trim my beard and edge my shit.

As I showered, I rested my palms on the tiled walls. All that flirting Cici did only reminded me that I didn't have a girl. The problem was I didn't want no shallow chick. The ones that tried to holla didn't have shit going for them. They wanted to live off me. All they were good for was eye candy when I wanted to go some- where and to fuck. The shit was pathetic. I spent a lot of time in Houston and Beaumont with Jasper, fucking shit up, and going to get parts for the shop, but no one had grabbed my attention.

I needed a woman that wasn't looking for somebody to be her knight in shining armor. Although, that was what my daddy was for my mama. She didn't have a pot to piss in or a window to throw it out of, but she was at least trying to better her situation by going to college. Even after she met my daddy, she finished her accounting degree, and now she was a vital part of the family business. I needed a woman that would add to me, not just suck me dry, figuratively speaking. She could definitely suck me dry in other ways. Every got damn day.

Nikki had already been by a couple of days ago and wore my shit out. But again, I could take that shit every day. Nikki was a chick I dealt with from Beaumont that knew just what this was. She wasn't looking for shit in life. I made sure I practiced safe sex with her at all times. For all I knew, she was probably hopping from my dick to the next. Every now and then, I'd break her off a few ends for gas. It was a thirty-minute drive from her house to mine.

Thinking about her had my dick rising, so I chose to focus on the type of woman I wanted. That was short-lived when I realized I didn't have a specific type. I didn't care about her size long as she was pretty, and she had to be doing something positive in her life, chasing her dreams and making her own coins.

As I washed myself, I could hear my phone ringing. I hurried it along, then got out to see I'd missed a call from my dad. Wesley Henderson was all about his business and was glad that all his children were the same way. I couldn't call him back now, though. Every conversation was at least twenty minutes long, and I had to be at Jasper's in the next fifteen.

# CHAPTER 3

## ASPEN

"I talked to Carlos. He told me you're going to Beaumont tomorrow."

*Bitch ass!* Whenever Carlos and I argued, he thought calling my mother was going to make matters better. That shit only made it worse. Our relationship should have been between the two of us. I wasn't a little girl that would get scolded by her mother. "No ma'am. I'm leaving today after brunch."

"Oh. I think he misunderstood, then. He thinks you're leaving tomorrow morning." She ate some eggs, then looked back up at me. "You know he hates when you travel alone."

He didn't have a problem with me traveling alone. He just didn't want me to work. "Mom, writing is my passion. Educating others about what's going on in our country is important to me as well. These people in Nome are losing their livestock and no one knows why. Nobody's investigating besides the locals. Something more needs to be done to further the investigation. People around this country benefit from their cattle."

She lifted her hands in the air. My mama hated confrontation. "I'm not against you, sweetheart. But why don't you wait until Carlos can go with you?"

"Because he never has time. This is gonna take me at least three days, but probably more. People don't easily trust outsiders."

"Just make sure you keep in touch with him while you're gone."

"I always do, Mom."

She smiled at me and continued eating her brunch. Truth was, I wasn't surprised he'd called her. He always did. What confused me was why I was letting the shit bother me. I was still gonna do what the fuck I wanted to do, and he could kiss my whole ass. As I picked over my eggs, I could see my mom watching me in my peripheral. She knew I wouldn't ever be happy with the type of arrangement Carlos wanted. Hell, he should've known that shit, too.

When we were done, I kissed my mom and told her I would call when I got to Beaumont. I had to go home and get my luggage. I hadn't planned on leaving today, so it was still in my bedroom. Just the thought of possibly seeing Carlos before I left had me on edge. Hopefully, he'd be gone. Usually, he and his friends played basketball on Sunday afternoons, so I was praying they were already gone. I hated the repeated arguments with him.

One day, I would gather up the nerve to just move the fuck out. It wasn't like I didn't have options. Being with Carlos was comfortable. I didn't have to worry about paying any bills or even cooking. Carlos handled everything. We had a chef, and a cleaning crew came in once a week. I cooked sometimes just to keep my skills up, but I did what I wanted when I wanted. It was like a paid arrangement. Carlos got sex when he wanted it and in return, I didn't have to do shit.

When I got home, Carlos was already gone, but I didn't have the heart to just leave without telling him. While I had fallen out of love with him, I still loved him, if that made sense. Carlos wouldn't be a bad catch for someone who had the same vision as he. Someone that wanted to be a trophy wife. I looked at my engagement ring and shook my head slowly. He'd proposed before I moved in with him, and I assumed he thought things would change. While in my mind, I thought things were going to get better.

After loading my suitcase, I called him. He answered immediately. "Hey, baby. We are just about to start our game. What's up?"

"I'm about to leave for Beaumont now instead of tomorrow. I need to be able to hit the ground running in the morning."

"Aspen... Whatever. Okay. Be safe."

Before I could respond, he'd ended the call. Oh, well. That wasn't going to make me stay. If he actually supported my career, then I probably would have cared if he got upset. Grabbing my luggage, I went to my Kia Optima and put it in the trunk, then got in the driver's seat. He hated this car, but it was a car that I bought with my own money. It also made people a little more comfortable with me. If I went researching in a Jag or Mercedes, people would think I was there to look down my nose at them. I looked at his picture on my screensaver, took a deep breath, then backed out the driveway.

———

ONCE I EXITED IH-10 ONTO HWY 90, I NOTICED THE URBAN, cement filled environment was disappearing and being replaced by grassy fields and less traffic. The last town I'd gone through that even resembled city living was Liberty, and it didn't even measure up. I was in a little town called Devers, and I saw a sign that said Nome was only a few miles away. Knowing the population, I knew that it was probably even smaller than the town I'd just passed through.

Within ten minutes, I saw a water tower and cell phone tower, then a sign that said welcome to Nome. Before I could look around, there was a loud popping noise and I nearly lost control of my car. I slowed down, but before I could turn on a side street, I could hear my rim meeting the pavement. *Fuck!* I couldn't mess my rim up in the middle of nowhere. There was a side lane in front of the post office, so I pulled over into it. I got out the car to assess the damage. My front passenger side tire had blown out.

Rubbing my hand down my face, I went back to the driver side and popped my trunk. Thankfully, my brother had taught me how to change a tire. The problem was, I hadn't done it since. Nor had I done it by myself. I didn't know how this was gonna work without me breaking my nails and messing up my clothes. After getting the tire, 4-way, and jack out of the trunk, I walked back to the side of the car. Pushing my glasses up on the bridge of my nose, I began trying to loosen the lug nuts. This shit was on here tight.

I was thanking God that it happened on the passenger side because cars were zooming by fast as hell. After I'd finally gotten two lug nuts loosened, I wiped the sweat from my brow. It was two o'clock in the afternoon, the hottest time of day. Just as I was about to start on the third one, someone tapped me on the shoulder, scaring the shit out of me. "My bad. I didn't mean to scare you. I just knew you heard this loud ass truck I'm driving."

I turned to look at him and my head fell backwards. This nigga was tall as hell and damn... he was sexy as hell, too. That thick beard, beautiful smile and tatted arms and chest had me mesmerized. He licked his lips, then asked, "You need some help, beautiful? You sweating out them fire ass curls."

"Umm... yes. Please? Thank you."

My hair was red on the ends, and my natural curls were probably turning to frizz in the humidity. I stepped to the side, then pushed my glasses up again. He watched me until I was out of his way, then gently grabbed the 4-way tire iron from my hand. "You did good. You changed a tire before?"

"Not really, but I've seen it done several times."

He nodded his head and proceeded to loosen the rest of my lug nuts like it was nothing. Watching the muscles in his shoulders was driving me crazy. Wife beaters should be outlawed. "You only have this lil donut?"

"Yeah, but I can get a new tire in the morning."

"You heading to Beaumont?"

After his questions, I started to think rationally. I didn't know him, and he could have ill intentions. Frowning slightly, I was about to tell him that it was okay. "My bad. You don't know me. I was just asking because I have a shop down the street."

"Oh. But my hotel is in Beaumont. How would I get there?"

He shrugged his shoulders as he proceeded to jack my car up. "What's up, Storm?"

We both turned toward the post office to see a man speaking. "What's up, Byron?"

"Your name is Storm?" I asked.

"Yeah. What's your name?"

"Aspen."

He took the tire off and put it in my trunk, then put the donut on and placed all the lug nuts on it, tightening them a little so he could lower the car. "I could bring you to Beaumont, but I could tell by the way you looked at me earlier you wouldn't be too comfortable with that."

I didn't know what to say. He tightened the lug nuts, then put everything in my trunk. "Follow me to my shop, and I'll get you a new tire on here now, instead of waiting for one of my techs to do it tomorrow."

I nodded my head, then got in the driver seat. Nervousness was infiltrating my body. Who was this guy? He probably didn't have a clue about the livestock issue that was going on. I'd probably still ask him though, because in the field I was in, you never judged a book by its cover. I was still somewhat nervous about going to this shop alone with him. Most places like that weren't open on Sundays, which meant it would be just him and me.

The shop turned out to be only a couple of blocks away, and as I turned in the driveway, another car turned in behind me. I sat there until a woman got out, along with an older woman. Hesitantly, I got out of my car as they walked past me to Storm. *What a sexy ass name.* "Your daddy wanted me to ask you if you could come by. We lost a bull today."

*Oh, shit! I hit the damn jackpot!* I walked over to them, and the

17

woman I assumed was his mother looked at me and smiled. "Hello."

"Hello."

"I'm sorry, Ms. Aspen. This is my mother, Joan, and my sister, Tiffany."

They both smiled at me, then looked back at him with smiles on their faces. There was obviously some type of silent communication going on. After opening the bay door and disarming the alarm system, Storm addressed his mother's concern about the bull. "Did he notice if anybody was around? Or anything unusual?"

"No, baby."

"Okay. Well, let me get her a new tire put on, and I'll be over there."

"Okay. See you, lil brother," his sister said, then gave me a smile.

They clearly had the wrong idea about what was going on. When they drove away, Storm had me drive into the bay. My nerves were back, although, my mind was telling me that I could trust him. As I got out of the car, his phone rang. "Hello...? What the fuck you on, Dre...? Naw, that's what happens when you try to screw somebody... Get the fuck outta here with that bullshit. You got off easy, so if I was you, I would tread softly before you get fucked up."

My eyes widened, and his lil conversation had my nerves on overdrive. He turned to me and said, "I'm sorry, Aspen. That was my punk ass cousin who didn't pay me for services rendered."

"It's... umm... It's okay."

He gave me a slight smile and went to work. As he did, I looked around his shop. It was a lot bigger than I expected. I wondered if he actually owned this place or if he was the manager. Managers always called the place of business theirs. They didn't seem to realize they were dispensable just like the rest of the staff. I walked over to a chair near the door to the waiting area and sat. "My bad. You wanna go inside to get some cool air?"

"No. It's okay. Can I tell you something?"

He stood up straight as the automatic lift hoisted my car in the air. "Yeah. What's up?"

"My name is Aspen St. Andrews. I'm a freelance journalist. I actually came out here to see if I could do a write-up on the mysterious deaths of livestock out here. I feel like it deserves more than local attention. I'm staying in Beaumont, but I planned to come back in the morning."

His eyebrows had risen, then he frowned slightly. "Well, I guess you hit the jackpot. You wanna follow me to my parents' land when I finish your tire?"

"Sure. How much will I owe you for the new tire?"

"Nothing, if you let me take yo' fine ass to dinner."

I was shocked by his forwardness. He had my ass on straight pause. However, my inner self was cutting flips and shit. "How much is the tire?"

"Will that determine the answer to my question?"

"No. I'm going to opt to pay for the tire."

"Oh, okay. My savage scared you, I guess."

"Let me tell yo' ass something, Storm. I'ma journalist, so I done seen it all. Yo' lil country ass ain't phased me. As you can see, I can get down just like you. I'm choosing to pay for the tire 'cause I don't know you. Secondly, I'm engaged."

I didn't know why I told him I was engaged. That shit sprang out of my mouth before I could stop it. I watched the one-sided smile appear on his face. "I guess I'll ignore those looks you giving me when you think I ain't looking, then."

*Shit.* He turned his back to me and continued changing my tire.

# CHAPTER 4

## STORM

God had to have a sense of humor. He dropped this damn goddess right on my path, only for her to be engaged. I could have *been* done fixing her tire a long time ago, but she had no clue that I was watching her on the monitor. She'd been watching me the entire time, tilting her head to the side and everything. She was thick as fuck, too. I should've known she was already taken.

Those green-rimmed glasses sitting on her nose were sexy as hell and her red-tipped, natural coils were giving a nigga a vibe that was unmatched by any other female I'd come in contact with lately. That was okay, though. I'd know by the end of the night if the nigga she was with was doing what he was supposed to, 'cause she was checking me out, for real. I knew women well, and she'd done everything but measured my dick. But if she kept looking at me like that, she'd be able to do that, too.

When I finished mounting her tire and making sure it was balanced, I unlocked the door so she could pay for the it along with my services. As she walked inside, she blew out fresh air as she took in the coolness. I told her to take her hot ass inside. She started spitting that slang, but I knew she had no clue of the hood life other than what she'd probably researched. I'd fuck her ass up and leave her all in her lil rich ass feelings. I could tell she came from money just by the way she was dressed. This was probably a hobby for her, just because she was nosy as fuck or some shit like that.

Most rich people felt entitled to shit. Like she was gon' bring her bougie ass out here and get all the information she wanted out of us and not do shit with it. My people were rich now, but we worked like we were still poor. I walked behind the register and proceeded to charge her, while she stood there silently watching me over the rim of her glasses. She was so fucking sexy, and I was willing to bet her fiancé didn't know what to do with all that shit. "Your total is $158.65."

She handed me her card, so I fake swiped it, then put it on the company credit card. I printed the receipt and handed it to her along with a business card. "Thank you, Storm."

"You welcome."

The way my name rolled off her lips had me ready to dig up in something. Nikki would have to do for tonight. I led her out to the bay again, then locked the door. Once I let her car down, she got in it and backed out so I could set the alarm and put the door down. When I got to my Chevy one-ton pickup, she put her window down. "Is it still okay for me to follow you?"

"Yeah."

I hopped in my truck. Obtaining female friends was never a goal of mine, so I didn't have any. I maintained a rough and rude demeanor, just so they didn't get confused. Since I'd flirted and she didn't bite, she was about to experience that nigga. The problem was that I was so attracted to her ass, and I knew she was attracted to me too, regardless of that small ass engagement ring on her finger. I never even noticed the shit until she said she was engaged.

I took off and she followed me down Highway 90 to Highway 326, and a couple of miles later, we were at my parents' land on Grayburg Road. I got out of the truck to see my daddy sitting on

22

the bed of his truck. One of the cows was found dead just yesterday. He scratched his head, then put his baseball cap back on. He looked stressed. I hated to see him that way. Jasper was sitting next to him, along with my other brother Kenny, the one who was part owner of the convenience store.

I turned my attention back to Aspen, then it immediately went to the heels she had on. Turning my head so I could chuckle, I turned back to see she'd come out of them and held them in her hand. I could no longer hide the grin on my face. Maybe she did know a lil something. City slickers didn't usually walk bare footed. When she'd gotten next to me, I proceeded to the gate. "Henderson is our last name."

"Okay. Thanks."

When I pushed the gate open, Aspen stepped right in some cow shit, and I could have died from laughter. But instead, I tucked my lips in my mouth and bit down on them as she rubbed her foot in the grass, trying to get it off. Looking up at my brothers, their faces were red from trying to hold in their laughter. That all came to a halt when my daddy chuckled. Once he did that, none of us could hold it in any longer.

Aspen looked up at us, and I could tell she was embarrassed. *Oh well.* I walked to my dad and brothers, shaking all their hands, then introduced her. "This is Aspen St. Andrews. She's a journalist who wants to do a write-up on the mysterious deaths of livestock in the area. Ms. St. Andrews, this is my dad, Wesley Henderson. He's the one you need to speak to."

Once I introduced the two of them, my brothers got up and let her sit on the tailgate with my daddy. The three of us walked away so they could take me to the bull that was dead. "Where's WJ?" I asked.

WJ, Wesley Jr., was the oldest. Normally, when something was going on, he was the first one out here. "Nesha had a meet. He's been out there all day."

Nesha was WJ's daughter. She ran track and was one of the fastest in the state. I nodded, then continued to see one of our biggest, meanest bulls stretched out on the ground. This shit was getting out of hand. This was the third bull we'd lost in three weeks. Lifting his legs, there was no gunshot to be found. I dropped them, then walked off to the feeding trough. "Jasper, you got any bags you keep yo' loud in?"

"Yeah, in my truck. Be right back."

That fool was a known weed head. He handled his business, though. I hit the shit with him every now and then. Out of all my brothers, I was the most knowledgeable about the animals. When I was younger, I stayed in the fields with Daddy and the vets that came out to work the cattle. That was why they all waited on me to come check things out. I knew so much about their care I could have become a veterinarian. It just wasn't in my heart though. I loved working on cars.

When Jasper came back with the small Ziplock bag, I dipped some of the feed out of the trough. This probably wasn't the problem, but it didn't hurt to be sure. This was the trough we used for the bulls. We only had a few bulls, so to lose three of them in less than a month was going to kill reproduction and overwork the last three we had in this field with almost seventy cows.

As I stood and shoved the bag in my pocket, I noticed Aspen watching me as my daddy talked in her recorder. She quickly averted her gaze back to my dad as I headed back toward my truck. "Yo, Storm. You know her?"

"Naw. She had a flat tire right in front of the post office."

"And Seven Storm Henderson had to come to the fucking rescue. Never took you as the save a ho type, Storm," Kenny said.

He was right above Jasper in age. "Shut the fuck up. She was there on that asphalt by herself. I own a damn tire shop. To walk past her would have just been cruel as hell."

"And? Everybody know yo' ass don't give a fuck," Jasper added.

"A'ight. I thought she was pretty, but she engaged, so. Fuck you, too, Jasper."

As I was about to walk to my truck, Daddy called my name. I

walked over to him and Aspen. "Did you find anything?" he asked when I got close.

"Naw. I just took some of the feed to sample. I doubt that's what the problem is, but I still need to rule it out. I'm going to Sour Lake with this. I'll be back."

"Okay, son."

He and Aspen continued talking as I hopped in my truck to go home and take a shower, then head to Sour Lake. Her intense stare while I was talking to my dad didn't go unnoticed. She was begging me to disrespect her lil relationship. I could see it in her eyes. This had gone beyond her initial reaction to me. She was damn near ogling a nigga. Before I could leave though, Jasper got in with me. "What, nigga?"

"She feeling yo' ass. She keep looking at'chu."

"Oh well. She can carry her ass on like the rest of these broads."

"You can fool everybody else, but I'm a rare breed, my nigga. You feeling her too, because you got way too much hostility in your voice to say y'all just met today."

"Maaaan, it's all physical. I don't know her to be feeling her."

"A'ight. Whatever. I'm going home and let this loud take me down."

"A'ight, bruh. I'll holla later."

He hopped out of the truck, and before I could back away, I saw my dad and Aspen looking my direction while still talking. I slightly rolled my eyes and hoped he wasn't telling her shit she didn't need to know.

---

AFTER SHOWERING AND GETTING THE SAMPLE TO A GUY I KNEW IN Sour Lake so he could analyze it for me, I was about to head back to see if my dad and Aspen were still on Grayburg talking, but a phone call halted my progress in that direction. It was Nikki. She must have sensed that I had thought about her earlier. "What's up, lil mama?"

"You know what it is, Storm. You busy?"

"Naw. Come on out."

"I'm on my way."

I bypassed Grayburg just in case they were still out there and kept going to Highway 90. Had I turned down Grayburg Road and passed by them without stopping, my daddy would have immediately called to see why I didn't stop. Once I got to my house on County Road 1009 and put in my gate code, my phone was ringing again. I hated talking on the phone. Most of my calls were short, but I would much rather text when I could. I saw my mama's number, so I answered. "Hello?"

"Hey, baby. You coming to dinner this evening?"

I looked at the time to see it was already almost five. Dinner was always at six. "No, ma'am. I'm drained. I'ma just chill at the house."

"Uh huh. I guess you forgot I know you. See you in the morning for breakfast then."

"A'ight, Ma."

Everybody knew that I fucked around, including my mama. Although it was something I refused to talk to my mama about, somebody had hipped her on game. Probably WJ's ass. He was a mama's boy, for real. By the time I got in the house and had gotten comfortable in some basketball shorts and socks, Nikki was buzzing the intercom at the gate. Time to fuck some shit up. I opened the gate up and allowed her to drive through.

I went to the back door and stood in front of the glass, storm door, looking at her fix her hair and put on more lipstick. I slowly shook my head. All that shit was about to get messed up. She was wasting her time, especially being that I didn't give a fuck about all that superficial shit. If a woman was pretty without all the makeup and hair and shit, that was what turned me on. All that other shit looked nice, but if we were fucking in the shower, I needed to be able to stand to look at her ass.

When she noticed I was watching her, she hurriedly got out of the car. Hopefully, she wasn't trying to be all intimate and shit. I just wanted to fuck and send her ass on. Every now and then, she wanted to take her time. I opened the door and allowed her to walk in. When I first saw that ass in Popeyes a few months ago, I knew I had to have it. By the way she'd looked at me, I knew she was gon' let me get it. And here we were. As she walked past me, I slapped her ass in those tights and watched it jiggle. "Oh, that's what'chu feelin'?"

"Ain't that what I'm always feeling?"

"Hell yeah."

She giggled as I closed the door, then turned around and picked her ass up and threw her over my shoulder. I hit those stairs two at a time to get to my room. Nikki's ass wasn't light, but I had that bionic strength when it was something or someone I wanted. I dropped her on my bed, then dropped my shorts. Before I could get to her, she was already on her hands and knees, ready to slob on my shit.

I didn't waste any time getting to her, either. With my dick in my hand, I guided it right where it wanted to be: in something wet, warm and sloppy. Fucking her mouth quickly, I needed to get that first nut out. My shit was throbbing, and I didn't want to keep him in pain any longer than necessary. I could feel her gagging on it and that just propelled me forward. She wasn't trying to pull away, so that was a good thing. This was where all that hair and shit irritated me. I couldn't even get a good grip on her hair because that shit was gon' come off.

I continued to guide her by holding the back of her head until my nut decided to join the party. My knees got weak for a second as the fluids left me, diving down her throat. After that shit, I almost didn't need to fuck, but I went ahead and strapped up while she cleaned her face. Now she was wiping all that makeup and shit on my towels. "Next time you come over here, come without all that shit on."

She frowned at me, but still came to my bed and tooted her ass

27

up. Before I could slide in, my phone started to ring. Noticing that it was only Jasper, I decided not to answer. I'd talk to him whenever. I dove into the second hole of hers and stayed the course; beating her pussy with every stroke as it talked back to me, telling me how much it loved what I was doing to it.

Slapping her ass as she tried to work that shit on me made me closer to nutting. Her shit felt good, but she was no good at trying to work my dick. I held her hips still as I power drove her shit, until I came in the latex.

Her screams helped me get there a little quicker, but I almost wanted to go a little longer just to relish the feeling. I pulled out of her and went to the bathroom to clean up. When I came out, she was still laying in my bed. "You gotta go, lil mama. You know the drill."

She huffed, then went to the bathroom and slammed the door. That shit pissed me off. I opened that shit and pushed her against the countertop. "I know you didn't slam my fucking door."

"Now, there's the muthafucka I like. Come give me that hurricane type shit, Storm."

This broad was crazy. But I was gon' give her what she wanted. I strapped up again and gave her that angry shit that pulled that fucking lace front right off her head. When I was gon' get through with her, she wasn't gon' be fit for shit but sleep. Unfortunately for her, she couldn't do that here.

# CHAPTER 5

## ASPEN

I awakened to the smell of eggs and bacon and was grateful the Henderson's had so graciously opened up their home to me. Mr. Wesley and Mrs. Joan said they would take me around to all the other ranchers that were losing livestock as well. This had been a lot easier than I thought it would be, and it was all thanks to Storm. Had I not run into him, I would be on my way to Nome, probably still trying to get people to talk to me.

When he left without saying goodbye yesterday, I felt a type of way about it. He was rude, but it didn't change my attraction. It was probably best that he stayed away. His arrogant attitude wasn't doing anything but fueling my fire. As I got up to get dressed and handle my hygiene, my phone began ringing. I immediately knew it was Carlos. "Hello?"

"Good morning. How was your trip?"

"It was good," I replied, knowing the bullshit was about to spew from his lips.

"Look. I'm sorry that it seems I don't support you in your career. I just don't want it to seem like I can't take care of you. I love you, Aspen. Maybe when you get back, we can sit and talk to make sense of things."

"Okay. Well, let me get going, and I'll see you when I get back in a couple of days."

"Aspen?"

"Yes?"

"You don't love me anymore, do you?"

"Carlos, we will talk when I get back."

"Alright. But if you no longer love me, then there's nothing that talking will do about that."

*Muthafucka, why are you still talking now, though?* "Carlos, we will talk when I get back," I said a little slower.

"Fine."

He ended the call. I huffed loudly, then went to the bathroom to prepare for breakfast.

Once I was dressed, someone was knocking on the door. I opened it to find Mrs. Joan. "Good morning, baby. Breakfast is ready."

"Thank you so much. I'm on my way down."

I went to get my purse and my phone. I'd pitched the story yesterday evening to Farm Journal Magazine, Farm World Magazine, and I planned to pitch it to World News. Farm Journal was all over it and couldn't wait to receive what research I had to offer. I had yet to hear from Farm World. There wasn't much information Mr. Wesley could give me other than the bulls were healthy.

He'd said that Storm was the one I really needed to talk to, and he couldn't understand why Storm had brought me to him. I had an idea why. According to Mr. Wesley, Storm was the only one that had taken a liking to the animals. He proceeded to tell me all the training he'd undergone from the veterinarians that had maintained the health of their livestock.

I'd kind of gotten that feeling yesterday when they were all sitting, waiting for him to arrive. Although he was the youngest, they all looked up to him when it came to taking care of the livestock. This man was the epitome of not judging a book by its cover. As I headed downstairs, I heard Mrs. Joan say, "You not staying, Seven?"

"Naw. I'm gon' head out to the shop."

The voice sounded a lot like Storm's. When I reached the bottom step, I saw him standing there with a plate in his hand. His eyes met mine, and he frowned. Ignoring his annoyance with me being there, I said, "Good morning, Seven."

Before he could advance toward me and say a word, his mom put her hand on his chest, holding him back. "Seven, have a good day at work, baby."

I guess I wasn't supposed to call him Seven. He was red as hell. Snatching his keys from the countertop, I quickly apologized. "I'm sorry. I didn't mean any harm. I thought your name was Storm."

"My name *is* Storm. Seven Storm Henderson. Only special people in my life are allowed to call me Seven. You aren't one of those people."

"Storm! Get out of here!" his mama yelled.

He didn't have to be so rude about it, but I guess that was my fault. I lowered my head as I stared up at him. His daddy came downstairs and asked, "What's going on?"

"Storm is being Storm. The winds are howling in here."

"Storm, I need you to take Ms. St. Andrews to the Daniels' property. Mr. Daniels said he would be willing to talk to her."

"Daddy, I need to get to the shop. I actually work, in case y'all forgot."

"Seven Storm Henderson."

"I apologize. I just have a lot of work to do today, Daddy."

Storm walked out the door as I sat at the table. It was like when he frowned at me, my whole body submitted to his authority. That shit was so damn sexy. My thoughts were a thing of the past when Mrs. Joan set those plates in front of me and Mr. Wesley. There was a whole pork chop on it. I'd never had a pork chop for breakfast. "I'm sorry, Ms. St. Andrews. Storm has always been a handful. I don't know where he gets his attitude from," Mr. Wesley said.

Before I could respond, Mrs. Joan interrupted. "Oh, I bet I know where he gets it from."

Mr. Wesley stuffed his mouth with grits, then shrugged his shoulders as I laughed. "It's okay. I shouldn't have called him Seven. He'd told me to call him Storm, and I should've stuck to that."

They looked at one another and smiled. I wasn't sure exactly what that meant, but I did know that I would be leaving tomorrow, if for nothing more than to get out of the eye of the hurricane. We ate our breakfast in almost complete silence. I could always get conversation going, but it seemed I had nothing in me to say. Storm had rendered me speechless, and that was something worth talking about.

Once we were done eating, Mr. Henderson said to give him an hour and he would be ready to take me to the Daniels, down on Nome Spur Road. After agreeing, I went to sit in Mrs. Henderson's sunroom in the front corner of the house. It was beautiful and there was a refreshing view of the pasture and the highway afar. Grabbing her crocheted blanket that was in the seat, I sat in her rocking chair, then draped it over my lap and closed my eyes. It was so quiet and peaceful. As I continued to rock, I could feel a presence. "Come on so I can take you to the Daniels's place."

I opened my eyes to see Storm standing over me. "Storm, I don't want to inconvenience you. If you'll just tell me how to get there, I could go by myself."

"No, you can't. The Daniels won't talk to you if one of us don't escort you. They'll actually run you off their property. The Walters's property is right down the road from theirs, so we'll go there afterwards. Let's go."

He walked away, so I quickly stood from my seat, dropping the blanket to the chair and followed him out. When we got to his truck, he opened the passenger door and walked off. I wanted to just stand there and wait on him to come back, but he probably would have backed out and left my ass. Thankfully, I was tall enough to climb in the truck. Once I'd gotten situated, I closed the door and buckled my seatbelt while he waited not so patiently. He turned around in the circle driveway and drove out the driveway.

It must have been a country thing that he didn't wear a seatbelt. Neither did his dad or either of his brothers yesterday. The inquisitive part of me wanted to ask why, but I decided to keep that to myself. The ride to the Daniels's was quiet as hell. The ride was only like five minutes, but I barely heard Storm breathing. After putting his truck in park, he got out in the gravel driveway and walked to the house. I opened the door and slid out the truck. Practically running to catch up with him, I said, "Storm, I really am sorry."

He didn't respond. After knocking on the door, he glanced over at me. "Be straight to the point. No bullshit."

A white man opened the door and he said, "Storm! What a pleasant surprise. I was expecting Wesley."

"Yes, sir. He sent me instead. This is Aspen St. Andrews. She's here to shed some light on the dying livestock. Maybe get us more attention so we can get some help trying to figure this out."

He was so proper just now. *Shit.* He could flip the script like that and still hold my attention? This was crazy as hell. I could barely focus now. "Okay. Yes. Ms. St. Andrews, do you mind sitting outside? My wife isn't home."

"That's perfectly fine, Mr. Daniels. I appreciate your time."

As we headed to the picnic table, Storm leaned against the post of the awning over the patio. "So, Mr. Daniels, how many cows have you lost?"

"Four cows and one bull."

"How long ago did the first one die?"

"About three weeks ago."

"Did you think anything of it? Or did you think maybe it was just a thing?"

"Well, I'd noticed the first one was hobbling the night before. So, I said to myself that I would have it checked the next morning. Well, when I went to check on it the next day, it was dead. I figured it had probably gotten bit by a snake or something. So, I didn't think anything of it until the next day when another one died."

"Have you been able to get the water, soil, or feed tested?"

"I got the water tested and it's fine. He said there was bacteria in it, but nothing serious enough to kill cattle. We've gotten that handled since then and changed all the filters. After that, we lost a bull and two more cows."

"That's strange."

"It really is. I feel like it's somebody that knows us in the area. Not many people know about this street unless they have people that live back here."

My interest was piqued. "You think someone is killing the live-stock? How?"

"I think they're being injected with something. I can't prove that, and I don't have the money for surveillance."

I turned to gauge Storm's reaction to what he'd said, and he was rubbing his beard, looking to be in deep thought. Mr. Daniels and I continued to talk about his suspicions, then we walked out to his pasture to look at the cattle. Storm didn't follow us, but I did notice he'd made a couple of phone calls. By the end of our conversation, Mr. Daniels hugged and thanked me for trying to get them some help.

When I walked back to where Storm was, he said, "Mr. Daniels hugged you."

"Yeah. He's sweet."

"He doesn't usually take to strangers so easily."

"Well, maybe I'm one of a kind."

"I guess," he said dismissively.

He walked off for the truck, so I followed along. We went down the road to the Walters' and their story of suspecting foul play was the same as Mr. Daniels's. They'd lost three cows. After finishing up my interviews, I was tired as hell. The heat had drained me, and I was sure my hair was a frizzy afro. I ran my hand over it as Storm not so secretly watched me. "Thank you for taking me where I needed to go, Storm."

"You're welcome."

"Are there any places to eat around here?"

"Not in Nome, but there are a couple of places in Sour Lake. Or you could go to Beaumont."

"How much further is Beaumont down Highway 90?"

"About twenty minutes."

"Listen. For some reason, I can tell that I annoy you. I haven't quite figured out why yet. But whatever the reason is, can I make it up to you and take you to lunch?"

His lip twitched like he was actually going to smile. I hadn't seen it since we were on side of the road yesterday. After I turned him down for dinner yesterday, he changed on me. I was sure I didn't make things look any better by being so eager to get information from him, when just yesterday I didn't want to be alone with him. "Storm…"

"Naw. I can't go to lunch. I need to check on my shop and do shit I put off this morning."

"Okay." I left that subject alone and moved to what his dad had said. "Your dad said that I should be talking to you about the livestock because you're more knowledgeable than he is."

"You won't get any more information from me than you got from him. I don't know what's going on."

"Okay. Well, is there anyone else that I may can talk to?"

"Naw, that's about it. There are a couple of others, but one is prejudice, and I would hate to go over there and fuck all his shit up and end up in jail."

I almost laughed, but he was dead serious. Clearing my throat, I said, "Well, I guess I can probably leave tomorrow. I thought I would be here longer."

He glanced at me, then asked, "Why did you think you would be here longer?"

"I guess I thought there would be more information about what ranchers thought was going on. Plus, I wasn't expecting everyone to be so friendly."

When we got to his parents' house, he didn't get out of the

truck. "Well, be careful going back to wherever you came from, Aspen St. Andrews."

"Thank you, Storm Henderson."

I slid out of his truck and closed the door. He peeled out before I even got to the front door. Hopefully, his parents were home. I wasn't trying to sit in my car until they returned.

# CHAPTER 6

## STORM

I hated being around Aspen that long. She was wearing down my defenses. When she said she was leaving tomorrow, I couldn't be more relieved. *That's a lie.* I was hoping she'd be here a few more days just to see her stare at and crave something she wanted but couldn't have. She was restricting herself because she was engaged, but obviously that shit wasn't what she wanted it to be. When I got to the shop, everything was flowing well, and there was only one car in the mechanic shop and Aston was almost done with it.

So, I headed home to take a shower and chill out for a minute. As I listened to Mr. Daniels talk, I called Jasper, Kenny, and WJ to tell them to keep their eyes and ears open. If somebody was going around injecting cattle, when I caught them, there would be no need for an article. I was gon' blow their fucking head off. I wanted to sleep on Grayburg Road, but there was nowhere to hide unless I slept under the shelter with the cows. I wasn't that damn desperate. Not yet, anyway.

My cell phone started ringing and I wanted to throw that shit. It had been on one all damn day. When I looked at the caller ID, I didn't recognize the number. Rolling my eyes, I answered anyway. "Hello?"

"Storm?"

"Yeah."

"This is Aspen. Your parents aren't home. Do you have a key to their house so I can take a shower and change?"

My mind immediately created a vision of her naked. I'd been doing my best to avoid lustful thoughts of her by telling myself, *Storm, she's engaged.* That shit wasn't working, though. "Yeah. Give me a minute to get dressed."

If I didn't hear her softly exhale, then I was tripping for real. "Okay."

Her voice was laced with that unfiltered, real shit. I didn't have a problem disrespecting her relationship if she didn't. I wasn't engaged to no-damn-body. Grabbing some jeans and a V-neck pullover shirt from my closet, I got dressed quickly. I sprayed a little cologne and put some lotion on my arms and hands. After brushing my waves and beard, I hurried out to meet Aspen's fine ass.

When I got there, she was sitting in her car. My parents were in Beaumont. They thought we'd be out longer. I knew what they were up to. Aspen obviously hadn't told them she was engaged to be married. Now that I thought about it, I didn't recall seeing that small ass shit on her hand today. I got out of my Range Rover and unlocked the door, then deactivated the alarm. She probably didn't know it was me since I wasn't in my dually. As I was walking back to my Range, she smiled. "I like that Range."

*Uh huh. That all you like?* "Thanks."

I leaned against it as she walked over. Everything in me wanted to grab her by her hips and pull her to me. "Can I take a look inside, Storm?"

"Yeah," I said as I stepped aside and opened the door.

"Ooooh, this is niiiiice."

I smiled, and she looked at me just in time to catch it. She gave me the fucking feels, and I hated that shit. "Thanks."

"Thank you for opening the door. You... umm... you going somewhere? You look nice."

"I thought that maybe I would take you up on lunch. I'll wait for you out here."

Her eyebrows rose, then she smiled. "Okay. We'll go wherever you wanna go. I'm gonna go shower."

She bit her bottom lip, and I almost followed her in that house. My parents wouldn't have been that happy if they walked in to see Aspen face down ass up on their Italian sofa. The thought of that shit caused me to chuckle. Since their asses wanted to try to set me up, I should give them something to see. Once Aspen closed the door, I got in my Range and waited for her to come out.

------

WHEN ASPEN CAME OUT THAT HOUSE, I WAS AMAZED AT WHAT she'd done in thirty minutes. Her skin was flawless. She only wore lipstick as far as makeup, and I couldn't be happier. The black pants and wrap around top had me drooling for a second. She had so much cleavage exposed I didn't know how I was going to keep my eyes on hers instead of her titties. Hopefully, I didn't offend her because I was a forward guy. I said what was on my mind and thought about that shit later... well not all the time.

Most times, I said what I meant and meant what I said. I didn't give a fuck what the other person thought about that. And Ms. St. Andrews was finna get the business, whether she liked it or not. I got out of the truck and looked her up and down while she blushed. "Damn. You look good as hell."

"Thank you."

I opened the door and grabbed her hand to assist her while she got in. She wasn't rejecting my advances this time. It made me wonder if it was because she wanted something from me. It didn't matter, though. I wanted something from her. I wanted to grab a hold of all that shit she called a body. Her weight was distributed just like I liked it. I didn't too much care for bad built women. If she was gon' have weight on her, I needed that shit to be all over, not just in one place. It may seem shallow, but oh well. I liked what I liked.

There was some heat in our touch, and I knew she felt that shit just like I did. Yeah, I had to have her. After closing the door and walking around to get in, she looked over at me and smiled. "So, what made you change your mind?"

"Honestly?"

I threw that warning out just for her. She didn't really know me like that. This was the only warning she'd get. "Yeah. Honestly."

"When you said you were leaving tomorrow, I knew that I couldn't let you leave without shooting my shot. That nigga you engaged to don't mean shit to me. You know why?"

She dropped her head, then stared up at me. "Why?"

"Because you been eye fucking me since you first saw me. So, he ain't doing something right. Secondly, you ain't got'cho lil pathetic ring on."

Her mouth opened, then closed again. She frowned slightly, but never looked up at me. I cupped her cheek and forced her to look at me. "I ain't tryna hurt yo' feelings, but I call it like I see it; unfiltered, raw and uncut."

"I see. So, where are we going?"

She was trying to change the subject and that was cool. That let me know that I'd read that shit to the tee. "I like the Olive Garden. That's cool wit'chu?"

"Yeah. I like the Olive Garden, too."

"Aspen, where you from?"

"Katy. Actually Houston, but we moved right after my senior year of high school."

"You and yo' dude live together?"

She seemed uncomfortable whenever I brought him up, but oh well. I was gon' ask the questions I wanted answers to. She fidgeted for a moment. "Yes."

I nodded my head and kept driving. Sliding my hand across the console, I grabbed hers, trying to steady her nerves. "What's he doing or not doing?"

She looked over at me for a minute. "He doesn't support my career. He wants me to sit at home and let him make the coins."

"You think it's something y'all can work out?"

"I don't know."

A one-sided smile made its way to my face. Yeah, she was gon' get all this shit I had to offer, even if she had to stay a couple of days longer. I was gon' convince her that she deserved a real nigga that could please her in ways she didn't even know existed. "So, check it. I need you to stay an extra couple of days. Let me show you all the shit you missing. If you ain't impressed, you can carry yo' ass back to Katy to that mediocre nigga you already got. No strings attached. But if you impressed, we got some shit to talk about."

She was real nervous now. Look like baby girl was trembling, 'bout to piss on herself. "Storm…"

"Naw. Just say okay, 'cause I ain't taking no for an answer. I'm finna snatch your soul. I already got yo' body, and I ain't even finessed that shit yet. You can't stop thinking about me and how I mentally stimulate you, with my rude ass. You can't hide that shit from me. I see it in your eyes. So, just let that shit go. You only gon' make weathering the storm hard on yo'self."

I watched her clench her thighs together from the corner of my eye. That pussy was mine. Now convincing her to leave that bitch made nigga in Katy would be the task. Aspen was silent the whole way to Beaumont. When we got to the Olive Garden and had parked, I looked over at her. "Aspen, look at me."

Hesitantly she did. "You didn't say okay."

"O… okay."

I pulled her to me and laid my lips on hers. She relaxed and accepted it until I slid my tongue against hers. Aspen pulled away from me so fast and hard, she fell against the door. "I can't do this. Storm… I'm engaged. I can't just let go until I figure out what I'm going to do about my relationship with Carlos. That isn't fair to him. Plus, I still don't know you. Not enough to go where you're trying to take it."

I chose to ignore her last statement, because her body was gonna voluntarily give me what I wanted. "Man, fuck him. How long y'all been getting into it over your career?"

She lowered her head. Maybe I was wrong about how easy this would be. But I wasn't gon' rest until I was deep in her shit, making her scream my name. She never answered me, so I got out of the Range and walked around to open her door. Aspen was a thinker and everything I'd said was flowing through her mind like oil circulating through a motor. I didn't have to be a rocket scientist to figure that shit out. I'd let her think.

She slid out of the SUV, and I grabbed her hand, glancing at her cleavage. That shit was speaking to me. Before we could walk away from the vehicle, I turned to her. "I get that you don't know me, but you about to."

She shuddered and that shit made me wanna scoop her ass up and have my way with her. She didn't have to worry. I was gonna bring all that shit out of her. Moving slowly was something I never thought about doing. When I saw something or someone I wanted, I dove all the way in. The moment I saw Aspen, I was fully submerged.

# CHAPTER 7

## ASPEN

S torm had my nerves in my fucking throat about to choke the shit out of me. When he kissed me, my panties got so wet I thought I'd pissed on myself. The shit he was telling me he was gon' do was turning me on so much, I didn't know what to do with myself. My body temporarily stopped listening to my common sense until his tongue invaded my mouth. Carlos's face had popped in my head. While I wasn't in love with him anymore, I owed him the verbalization of that. I felt like I was cheating on him. Technically, I was. That shit had me feeling disgusted with myself.

We walked inside the restaurant, and the hostess immediately sat us in a booth. I ordered some wine to ease my nerves while Storm stared at me from across the table. He had my nerves frazzled to say the least. It was even hard to look back at him. My body wanted him, and I didn't know how to reel the shit between my legs back in. She'd jumped all the way in upon sight. That was crazy as hell, because I hadn't been with another man in almost four years. She was supposed to only be for Carlos, but here she was entertaining the thought of another man gracing her walls... a man we didn't even know!

The waitress brought out my glass of wine and introduced

herself to us and asked if we wanted appetizers. Storm ordered some spicy shrimp, and I declined. Then, I chose soup instead of salad, and he did the same. I gulped my wine and saw the smirk that appeared on Storm's face. Finally finding my voice, I asked, "How old are you?"

"Twenty-eight. You?"

"Thirty-one."

He bit his thick bottom lip as his eyes slid down to my cleavage. It was so hot in this damn restaurant. I shifted in my seat and tried my best to calm my horny ass down. "So, how old were you when you started your shop?"

"Twenty-four."

His answers were extremely short, and I knew where he wanted the conversation to go. "So, what do you like to do in your free time?"

He thought for a minute, then glanced at the empty booths around us. "I like watching movies."

"That's it?"

"I like to fuck too."

My face had to have turned fifty different shades of red. I should have known better. One thing I'd learned quickly was that Storm spoke his mind, no matter how tactless. I made a mental note to try not to ask open-ended questions. "Aspen, why you red? You don't like to fuck?"

I put my hand over my face. He was fucking with me, and I was starting to take offense to it. "Why are you being an ass?"

The waitress brought our soup and bread sticks, along with his spicy shrimp. She took our dinner orders, and I only ordered a salad. Then I realized as long as I was angry with him, I could control my desires. I frowned as I took a spoon of my soup. I continued to eat although Storm was staring at me the entire time with that sexy ass smirk on his face. "I guess you mad. You asked the question, so how you gon' get pissed at my response?"

"Because you could be more tactful than that. You don't know me, Storm."

44

"Your name is Aspen St. Andrews… a thirty-one-year-old free-lance journalist from Katy by way of Houston. You come from money. I can see that shit a mile away. You're also a thinker. You like to analyze shit instead of just going with the flow. You're confident and you know you're sexy. Faking shit is how you get by, just like you're acting like you don't want to fuck me right now. I see that shit in your eyes and your body language. When you were clenching your thighs together in the Range, I knew you wanted me. Why you think I kissed you? You wanted that shit. Then you let that nigga back home fill your thoughts and doubt what was going on between us."

I was sitting there with my mouth slightly open. How in the hell was he able to read me like that? Carlos never could do that shit. "Something else I know, Ms. Aspen. You like to fuck just like I do."

He laughed when I frowned, then took a spoon of his soup. "What'chu know about me?"

"You're an arrogant jackass."

"That's it? That's all you know?"

He chuckled as I took a spoon of my soup. I decided to go there with him, since he wanted to play. "Your name is Seven Storm Henderson. You don't like people who aren't close to you to call you Seven for some reason. Maybe your mom will tell me why."

He was frowning now. "My, my, my. How the tables have turned."

Storm sipped his lemonade as I continued. "You're a twenty-eight-year-old business owner from Nome. You grew up on the farm and love animals. You practically know as much as the vets but didn't want to go to school for it. You love fixing cars. That's your passion. You get quiet when you're pissed but will definitely speak your mind if provoked. According to your mother, you can be downright hateful at times. So just remember, Storm, you aren't the only one that can speak their mind and have a nigga on hush."

He nodded his head. "Well, it seems like we do know each

other. So, maybe now you can have the courage to tell ol' dude back home that you aren't in love with him anymore."

I rolled my eyes. The waitress finally brought out my salad, so I asked for a box. Storm was someone I needed to get away from. I needed to remain levelheaded, and he was threatening to have me so angry and wide open, that we'd end up fucking today. That couldn't happen. "You can get a box all you want, Aspen. We aren't leaving until I'm done eating."

"Well, that's the magic of Ubers. I don't have to wait for you, Seven Storm Henderson."

"Make sure you leave some money to pay for this lunch you invited me to, then."

He was tap dancing on my last nerve, but I was still turned on. That shit was making me even angrier that I was still feeling him with all his antics. I stood from the booth and dropped a bill on the table. I grabbed a breadstick from the basket and said, "And you can keep the salad."

I felt good about myself as I walked away and called for an Uber. That shit was short-lived and somehow, I believed he knew what I didn't. No one would bring me to Nome. I was going to have to eat my words to get back. I couldn't go back to that table, though. Maybe I should have been grateful for what I had in Carlos. If this was what the dating scene was like these days, I would be fucked. I sat on the bench, thinking about my life, then decided to text Carlos. *See you tomorrow.*

He texted back immediately, like he was waiting for me to reach out. *Okay. I miss you.*

As I sat there, steaming because I was gonna have to wait on Storm to eat all that food, his brother Jasper walked in. He'd joined me and his parents for dinner last night. "What's up, Ms. St. Andrews. You need a ride back to Nome?"

I frowned slightly. Storm had to have called him. "Umm… yeah."

I stood to my feet, then glanced back toward where I knew Storm was still sitting, then followed Jasper out to his car. He opened the door to his Mercedes G Wagon, and I slid inside. Storm had been such an ass, but I felt soft toward him since he'd called his brother to come get me. He cared enough to not let me sit there and wait on him. Before Jasper got inside, he was on the phone with someone but ended the call before getting inside. "I see you got the salty side of the Storm."

He chuckled after he said it, causing me to assume that Storm always had this problem with women. I rolled my eyes. "He's extremely arrogant."

"Yep."

"He's a jackass."

"Yep."

"He's sexy."

"Yep... whoa, whoa. Hol' up. That nigga a'ight. You caught me slipping."

"Why is he like that? He just says whatever he wants, and I'm supposed to be okay with it. He has no tact, and I'd had enough."

"He told me. He's always been that way."

"What do you mean, he told you?"

"He said he pushed too hard. That he likes you, but you're engaged. For him to admit that to me, you got to him."

I lowered my head, looking at my nails. Did I give up too soon? No, I didn't. Just because he was sexy didn't mean I had to put up with his disrespectful, rude ass. Tomorrow I would be out of here and back to my uneventful life. As true as those words were, it did nothing to lift my spirits. "Jasper, stop the car."

"What?"

"Bring me back."

He frowned, then smiled. "Aww shit. You finna go tell that storm, peace be still, huh?"

My mouth opened slightly, but before I could respond he fell out laughing. I couldn't help but join him. I could clearly tell that he was the jokester of the family. He whipped his car around and drove the five minutes back to the restaurant. As he pulled up to the door and I'd thanked him, Storm was coming out with a to-go bag. He stopped when I got out of Jasper's car. Walking over to him, I asked, "Is it cool if I ride back with you?"

He smiled slightly, then wrapped his arm around my shoulder and kissed my head. We headed to his ride, and he asked, "Why did you come back?"

I almost let what Jasper told me slip from my lips, but I knew he wouldn't be happy with Jasper if I did. "I don't know. Are you gonna make me regret it?"

"Naw. I pushed you too hard." He stopped walking and gently cupped my cheek and rubbed his thumb across it. "My bad."

I nodded, and we continued to his SUV. He seemed so tender now, and I couldn't help but wonder if this nigga was bipolar. After opening my door, he grabbed my hand, assisting me. I watched him do what he'd been doing all afternoon... glancing at my cleavage. Maybe I should've rethought my wardrobe choice. My damn titties were so big, any shirt I wore would've shown cleavage.

When Storm got in the vehicle, he started up and drove away without a word. Our entire ride to Nome was quiet. I didn't know what to say to him. This afternoon had been somewhat of a disaster. Since I wouldn't be getting any more interviews done, I might as well head home today. It was only three o'clock. I would still be home before it got dark. Before I could get out of his vehicle, he grabbed my hand. "Thanks for coming back."

He kissed it, then pulled me closer to him and kissed my lips. My eyes closed for a moment, and when I opened them, he was smiling. I couldn't help but smile back. "I know I fucked up my chance by being entirely too forward. So have a safe trip back to Katy."

I eased out of the SUV and felt a sense of sadness come over me. Once I was out, I stared at him for a moment and swallowed hard. I gave him a slight nod, then closed the door. His parents looked to be back home, so I headed to the front door to find it unlocked. When I opened it, Storm drove away, leaving me reeling in my thoughts, barely knowing which way was up.

# CHAPTER 8

## STORM

Clearly my rough, forward approach wasn't compatible to Aspen's sweet, somewhat reserved personality. She wasn't the type of woman I was used to, although, I felt like she was the type of woman I needed. After going by the shop again and picking up the bank bag to head to Sour Lake to make a deposit, I headed home. As I did, I passed in front of my parents' house to catch a glimpse of Aspen loading her car. Damn, was I that bad?

Everything in me wanted to turn in their driveway and find out why she was leaving today instead of tomorrow like she'd originally said, but my pride had me drive on by. I dropped the lock bag back to the shop, since I'd forgotten the other one at home. Now that Aspen was leaving, maybe I could concentrate on what the fuck I was supposed to be doing. I just knew I had her when she said okay to my proposal. I'd planned to fuck her world up for the next two days, wining and dining her and showing her a side of me many people didn't get to see.

Only one woman had seen that side of me, but unfortunately, she wasn't here to tell about it. Amber was killed in a bad car wreck at the main intersection here in Nome. A truck had run the red light on Highway 90 and plowed into her. She was in ICU for a week, fighting for her life, but she ended up losing the battle. She was also the last woman to call me Seven. I grieved her death for a while, mainly because we were on bad terms when she died. I never got a chance to make it right with her. It was my fault as usual, for being an ass.

She was a beautician, and I'd jumped all over her for braiding this nigga's hair that I knew from school. I couldn't stand his ass, and Amber knew that shit. We all had gone to high school together. Garrett and I had gotten into it over a girl in ninth grade, then again in eleventh grade over a different girl. Finally, I got the opportunity to beat his ass in eleventh grade and shit between us slowed down for a minute. By senior year, I was with somebody else, and that nigga tried to fuck with her too. He just didn't have the sense God gave him.

People started calling me Storm because I had had enough of that muthafucka. I walked the halls with my 270 deer hunting rifle, ready to blow his fucking head off. Had Mr. Abney not talked some sense into me, he would have been a goner, and I would have been in jail for murder. I got suspended for three days, and they allowed me to come back. When I went back to school, Garrett's ass avoided me like the plague.

It was a good thing I was in a school that was lenient with their students. My family's name helped a lot too. They were lenient because everybody knew everybody. They knew what type of kids they were dealing with. I wasn't a troublemaker, but I wasn't gon' just keep letting that nigga disrespect me either. The situation was swept under the rug, but the kids that saw it didn't have a problem spreading the news.

So, when Amber was braiding that muthafucka's hair, that shit set me off. I'd seen him walking out of her shop in Beaumont. I'd made a trip out there to get parts to fix my friend's car and was passing by on my way back to Nome. When I saw that, I bust a U-turn in the middle of College Street. I stormed in Amber's spot, and she damn near jumped out her skin. We argued in front of her customers, and I came close to grabbing her ass. The next day, the accident happened.

When I got home, I got a beer from the fridge and relaxed. Before I could get settled good, my phone was ringing. I already knew it was Jasper calling to see how things went. "What's up?"

"You tell me. I was surprised as hell when she asked me to bring her back."

"Ain't nothing up. I halfway apologized for being an ass and dropped her back to Mama and Daddy house. She left today instead of waiting 'til tomorrow."

"Damn, bruh. I know you was feeling her or at least wanted to get to know her."

"Yeah, but it's cool. What'chu doing?"

"What I do best, besides cut hair."

"A'ight. After I eat, I'm coming over, so have my loud ready."

"Yeah, you wanted her ass."

"Whatever, nigga."

I ended the call with him still talking noise and continued drinking my beer, wishing I could have been hugged up to Aspen by now. Her kiss was everything I thought it would be… sweet like honey and her lips were soft as hell. Even though I could feel her nervousness through them, they were mine for that moment. I got up and warmed my food from the Olive Garden and ate. When she'd left earlier, she'd taken my appetite with her. I'd finished my shrimp and ordered a crown and coke, then had my food boxed up.

As I enjoyed my shrimp fettucine alfredo, my phone chimed with a text message. *Hi, Storm. I decided to leave today instead of tomorrow. Thanks for everything. I noticed that you never charged me for the tire, and you somehow slipped the hundred-dollar bill I'd left on the table for lunch into my purse.*

I read her message a few times. Damn, I hated that I fucked things up. But did I want a woman that was so sensitive? Yeah, I did. I wanted her. She was only that way because we had only been around each other a couple of days. I responded, *You're welcome.*

I didn't know what else to say without sounding sensitive and shit, so I left it at that. I grabbed another beer from the fridge and downed it quick as hell, then headed to Jasper's house.

---

"YEAH, MA. HE'S HERE... I DON'T THINK NOW IS THE BEST TIME for that."

Jasper was on the phone with Mama. She'd called me a couple of times, but I had no desire to talk about Aspen to her, so I didn't answer. I took a pull from the blunt my brother had waiting on me. It was doing a good job of numbing my insides. The feelings I had swirling around inside of me hadn't been felt since I first met Amber.

I moved fast when I felt strongly for someone, and I didn't know any other way to be. Maybe people always giving me what I wanted had spoiled me, but I knew what I was feeling from her. Aspen was just afraid to act out on it. She wanted me as badly as I wanted her, and because of that, I could only hope that she would be back.

She had my number and knew how to find me. However, she could work things out with her nigga. If she did, then I wouldn't have a choice but to let go of the hope that she would return to me. Jasper had finally gotten off the phone with Mama and was shaking his head. "What?"

"She thinks y'all are so perfect for each other."

I rolled my eyes and took another pull. "Nigga, pass that shit."

I frowned at him. "This shit was supposed to be mine, nigga. I ain't sharing shit. I'm sure yo' stash ain't low."

"Oh, that's how you do me? I'm the one supplying the shit! Wait 'til I tell Mama how you really feel about Aspen."

"Don't make me fuck you up like I almost did your bum ass cousin the other day."

"Who?"

"Dre bitch ass. I replaced a fucking transmission for his ass and only charged him $500. That muthafucka had that nerve to complain and only gave me $300. Before I pulled his truck out, I went under that bitch and cracked his oil pan."

"Dre a free-loading ass nigga that'll try to get over. You know that muthafucka got me on a cheap ass haircut?"

I couldn't help but chuckle. When a nigga couldn't even pay fifteen dollars for a haircut, he needed to reevaluate his fucking life. Jasper was all fun and games, but he didn't bullshit when it came to his money, whether it was fifteen dollars or fifteen grand. "So, what'chu gon' do about Aspen?"

"Nothing. What is there to do? She engaged."

"But she obviously feeling something for you, Storm. I could see that shit in her eyes."

"The ball is in her court. I put all my cards on the table earlier. I wanna show her what it means to be that dude in her life. But she's already taken."

I shrugged my shoulders and took the last pull off the blunt while Jasper stared at me for a minute. He knew it had been a while for me to even want something more than pussy from a woman. He also knew for me to admit that was huge. The rest of our conversation was light, and we decided that we would do something this weekend that we hadn't done in a long time: go fuck the club up. As we planned our weekend in Houston, my phone rang. I looked at it to see it was my daddy. "Hello?"

"I found another one in the back field. It's obviously been there a while. The buzzards done damn near demolished it."

"A'ight. I'm on my way."

If somebody was rustling, that shit was still on the books in Texas that it was punishable by hanging. They may not be enforcing that shit anymore, but I would be. Whoever was doing this shit was gon' get hung by their balls when I caught up with him. Man or woman, if they were coming out at night, roping cattle to inject them with whatever, they had big ass hairy balls.

"Another one?" Jasper asked.

"Yeah, one we most likely overlooked. The buzzards done had a field day with it."

"I'ma ride out there wit'chu."

"A'ight. Let's go."

---

"This shit is jumping tonight!"

"Hell yeah."

Jasper and I were in Houston at Aura turning up, watching all the ass that was shaking. The week had sped by and had been uneventful. Thursday night, I'd slept outside just to try to catch somebody slipping on our Grayburg property. Of course, just because I was out there, nobody tried anything. As soon as I left the shop today, I went home and took a shower. Nome had gotten old, and I wanted to just have fun tonight, or at least watch other people have fun.

We were seated in VIP, so ass was shaking naturally for us. Jasper was having the time of his life and that kept me entertained. I'd gotten a couple of lap dances like this was a damn strip club, but I'd mostly been drinking. While I was somewhat tipsy, I thought I saw a familiar face. There was no telling, though, because I was high, too. Jasper and I smoked the whole hour it took us to get to the club. He was more of the smoker, so that shit didn't even bother him. But me? I was high as a giraffe's ass.

I could have sworn I saw Aspen, though. She'd been on my mind all week, and the night I'd slept outside, thoughts of her had given me sweet dreams. No woman had ever plagued my mind as much as she had. I relaxed on the couch and put my feet up on the ottoman and drank my Crown while Jasper danced with some nasty ass looking chick. I turned my lip up. She looked like she smelled like ass. Gulping the rest of my drink, I stood to go drain the monster.

When I did, I saw Aspen. I knew that was her ass. She was with a group of women, and one looked to be getting married. She had on a crown, and she wore a sash across her body. I decided that I wouldn't bother her. If she saw me, then cool. If she didn't, that was still cool. As I headed to the restroom, this chick stopped me in the hallway. "Slim?"

"Naw."

"My bad. You kinda look like him."

I'd heard that shit almost my whole damn life. She'd gotten me confused with the rapper, Slim Thug. I believed that shit had a lot to do with my height and my complexion, because to me, we didn't look a thing alike. "So, what's your name?"

"Storm. Lil mama, let me take a piss. I'll be out in a minute."

She saw me trying to get to the restroom. Why would she keep talking? *Inconsiderate ass.* When I started pissing, it was like that shit didn't wanna stop. That was the only thing about drinking, that I didn't like. I stayed my ass in the restroom, which made it extremely hard to get drunk. I'd have to consume a lot within a short amount of time. When I finally came out, lil mama was still standing there. "What's up, shawty? What's your name?"

"Candace, but everybody calls me Candy."

"That right? You sweet like candy too?"

"That's what I hear."

She followed me to my seat, so I bought her a drink. She was cute enough, at least under these damn club lights. Hopefully, that shit didn't change if she was so lucky to leave with me. I wasn't talking much to her, but she was almost holding a full-fledged conversation by her damn self. I gave her one-word responses. As I sat there watching Jasper finesse some chick, grabbing all on her ass and shit, Aspen appeared right in front of me. "Storm! Hey!"

"What's up?"

I didn't stand to greet her, so she sat next to me and pulled me to her for a hug. I couldn't help but take in her scent. "Damn, Aspen. You smell good."

She blushed and it was then that I could see she was tipsy just like me. Ol' girl sitting next to me cleared her throat like I owed her something. I frowned, then looked at her and waved her off. "You can go."

She smacked her lips and gave Aspen a look, then left. *Yeah bitch, move around.* She'd better be glad Aspen was even there, or I would have told her that shit. She was a sack chaser anyway. Her ass was barking up the wrong fucking tree, though. Looking back over at Aspen, I asked, "So, what 'cho high saddity ass doing here?"

She rolled her eyes, then laughed. "Ain't nobody saddity, Storm. But... one of my friends is getting married. We aren't that close, but I figured I needed to get out the house."

"Why you needed to get out the house?"

I knew why I needed to get out, but that shit didn't matter now. I'd been trying to get my mind off her all week and finally wasn't thinking about her tonight until I saw her. She shrugged her shoulders. I knew what the deal was. She was thinking about me, too. Sliding my hand down her arm, I grabbed her hand and bit my bottom lip.

She looked so sexy tonight in a black spandex dress and a denim jacket. Her curves were intoxicating. "You look sexy as fuck, Aspen."

She eased her hand from mine, so I assumed she was still on her shit about me being too forward until I saw a chick walking toward our section. "Aspen, I was wondering where you went. Who's this?"

She eyed me, looking me up and down. Aspen got annoyed. I could see that shit all over her, and it made me chuckle. She didn't want to act on what was going on between us, but she didn't want another female giving me attention either. "What's up, shawty? I'm Storm."

"Well, damn. What kind of Storm?"

"A whole shit storm. Total devastation."

Aspen was steaming, but if this was what it took for her to give into me, I could do this shit all day. "Well, damn. I almost thought you were Slim when I first walked up. How do you know Aspen?"

"She interviewed my dad about his mysteriously dying cattle almost a week ago."

"Cattle? You a country nigga?"

"Hell yeah. What'chu know about it?"

Maaaan, Aspen had done turned red as hell. When shawty sat on the other side of me, she was about to leave. I grabbed her hand, pulling her back down next to me. "I don't know shit about it, but I would sure like to find out."

"I bet you would. You look like you more my brother speed, though."

She looked over at Jasper and smiled. Jasper was a'ight looking. I mean, he was my brother. "Oh, I see. You got your eye on Aspen."

"Naw. I got my eye on my business, where your eye should be."

She frowned at me, then walked off while Aspen tried to leave again. "Why you tryna leave?"

"Because... I didn't need to witness that."

"Why not? Something you ain't telling me?"

She folded her arms across her chest, not wanting to say what she was feeling. I smirked, then ordered another drink. She didn't know it yet, but she was gon' give in eventually.

# CHAPTER 9

## ASPEN

The last person I was expecting to see in the fucking club was Storm. He looked so damn good in his slacks and black button-down. I couldn't focus on anything else when I saw him, so I decided to go speak. What I didn't count on was getting all in my damn feelings because Sharae came looking for me and started flirting with him. Storm wasn't mine. Why in the fuck was I tripping? The crazy thing was that he was getting a kick out of the shit.

The DJ decided to spin a joint from Chris Brown's new album, and Storm surprised me when he turned to me and asked, "You wanna dance?"

I uncrossed my arms, then glanced around like he was talking to someone else. "Really?"

"I asked, didn't I? Come on."

He stood to his feet and pulled me to mine. When he stood behind me as I started dancing, my body heated up tremendously. Then, he rested his hands on my hips and all I could think about was him hitting it from behind. I closed my eyes for a moment, getting totally lost in the moment, twerking my shit on him. That Patrón running through me had me in rare form and Storm was getting to see it all. As I danced, his grip on me got tighter, and he spent me around to face him.

He grabbed my ass and that shit felt so good. Resting my hands on his shoulders, I began working shit out. The lower I went to the floor, the lower my hands slid down his body. Before long, I was eye level with his crotch and holding on to his waistband. I looked up at him and licked my lips as he stared at me. He was giving me the look. The same look he gave me in his Range that day we went to Olive Garden.

Grabbing my hands, he yanked me up and spun me around. His arms were wrapped around me, and my body was pressed against his. That erection he was sporting was driving me crazy. I should probably tell him that I was no longer engaged and that I would be moving into my own place next weekend, but I knew if I did, there would be no way he would let me leave alone tonight. No one knew that I'd broken off the engagement with Carlos, but that was no one's business, either.

When I'd gotten home Monday evening, Carlos and I had talked immediately upon my arrival. He didn't even let me get unpacked before he'd gone right in. The conversation started off lovingly, like he was going to be okay with my career, then it suddenly went to how embarrassing it was for people to think that I *had* to work. After I asked him why I couldn't work because I wanted to, he got an even bigger attitude. Telling me how his mama was right about me and that I wasn't wife material. That shit pissed me off so bad, I told him well, maybe not, so here's your ring back. I also proceeded to tell him that I hadn't been in love with him for a while.

The argument ended with me telling him that I would be moving out and him storming out the house and slamming the door. The next day, we discussed keeping this split to ourselves until we worked out a settlement of what was rightfully mine from our relationship. I could care less about all that shit he bought. I had no intentions of taking anything I didn't buy. We agreed we would tell our parents next weekend once I moved out. Breaking me away from my thoughts, Storm pushed my hair to one shoulder, then leaned down to my ear. "Keep this shit up, you gon' be coming home with me. Fiancé be damned. If I would have known you danced like this, I would have never asked. This shit is torture."

After he finished talking, he kissed my neck. My body was already hot, but that shit went up in flames when his lips came in contact with my neck. Gazing out into the crowd, I could see the women I came with staring at me. *Great.* While I was now single, no one else knew that. I was almost sure Carlos would know about this before I even got home. Turning to face him, I stopped dancing, then went sat down on the couch where we were.

Storm stared at me for a minute, then came to the sofa, too. "What's wrong? I'm wearing that ass down, huh?"

*Hell yeah.* He'd worn my ass down upon sight. I wanted to give him just what he wanted when I saw him. I rolled my eyes, then glanced over at the crew, watching me. "Ooooh. They gon' go back and tell your settlement."

"What?"

"The nigga you settled for."

"Storm, at one time, I did love him. So, I didn't settle. You don't know shit about that situation."

"So, now you defending the nigga? You wasn't thinking about him when you was twerking that fat ass all over my dick a minute ago."

"You know what? I don't know why I came over here."

"Yeah, you do. I'm saying all the shit you thinking. You wanna go somewhere private? I'm down for that, too."

"I'm sure you are. I'm not fucking you, Storm."

"You said that to convince yourself? 'Cause that shit was weak as hell and it shol' wasn't convincing."

I stood, and before I could walk my dizzy ass away, Storm pulled me to his lap and ran his hands up my thighs. "You feel this shit? How you gon' walk away from it twice? You make it a habit of denying dick?"

"Only dick that isn't mine, jackass."

"But it could be yours. All you gotta do is say the word. I'll have you taking dick all night tonight. You done made me horny as fuck, girl."

Feeling his hands roam my body had paralyzed me. I'd almost let out a moan. Quickly standing to my feet, Storm stared up at me. He was drunk as hell. I was tipsy, but he was gone. "It was good to see you, Storm."

He smirked, then moved his legs so I wouldn't trip. I really didn't want to leave, but I knew I needed to. *Why did I need to?* As I pondered that in my tipsy state, Storm grabbed my hand. "Just chill with me. We ain't gotta do shit. I'm just fucking wit'chu 'cause I know it bothers you. Sit down, girl. Worry about that nigga when you get home. The damage already done."

He was right. I'd done enough for him to be pissed. Me sitting with Storm wasn't gon' make things any worse. So, I did just that as he draped his arm across the couch behind me.

---

"So, I guess you were living your best life, tonight."

Carlos scared the shit out of me. I just knew he would be asleep. I'd sat with Storm until two, then decided to take the hour drive home. He and Jasper had offered to take me, but they were worse off than me. Storm and I had talked so much. His drunken state had him sensitive as hell. Shit he probably wouldn't have ever told me, he let loose. Even his last girlfriend that had gotten killed in a car wreck. I felt horrible for him, and I now knew why he didn't want me calling him Seven. He still wasn't completely over her.

To know I was the first woman he'd wanted to be with since then made me feel special as hell. I'd told him all about my relationship with Carlos. I'd even ended up telling him that we weren't together anymore, but still living together until I moved out next weekend. When I told him that, he'd grabbed my hand and his eyes held so much hope in them. I didn't know how to take that. He'd even offered to help me move. I liked his sensitivity tonight. It was his soft side that he'd tried to keep hidden from everyone. But he'd shown it to me.

"What are you talking about, Carlos?"

"Who was the guy you were with in the club? I thought you were going to a bachelorette party?"

"I did go to a bachelorette party. I just happened to see an acquaintance and decided to talk to him."

"You must be extremely talented to hold a conversation while you were twerking all over him, practically fucking him on the dancefloor."

"Carlos, we aren't together. Remember?"

"Yeah, but we agreed we wouldn't announce our breakup until next weekend when you moved out."

"Why? This shit ain't no engagement. We broke the fuck up. That ain't gotta be an announcement. I'm sick of this bougie shit," I said, letting my proper tone take a vacation.

His eyebrows had risen. I'd never engaged my hood voice on him, but he was fucking with my nerves. I was in a great mood before I got here, but now, I was almost ready to call Storm to see if I could meet him and Jasper in Nome. "So, is that how you talk when you aren't around me? Forget your fucking home training? Lose all your etiquette training and dignity? I'm glad we aren't getting married, because I don't know who you are right now."

He stood from his seat on the couch and went to the bedroom. I was glad he decided to end the conversation. All I wanted to do was take a shower and lay in bed and text Storm. When I got to the guestroom, I pulled my phone from my purse and did just that. *I'm home. Have y'all made it back to Nome?*

*We're about ten minutes away. I'll text you after I take a shower.*

*Okay.*

I set the phone on the nightstand, then went to take a shower myself. Hopefully, I didn't fall asleep before he hit me back.

Knowing that it was possible that I might see him again next weekend had me happy as hell. The arrogant jackass had a sensitive side. Who knew? In those moments, I hung off his every word. Although I knew he was drunk, I knew that was the real him. I was always told that a drunk man didn't tell lies, and I believed every word he'd said tonight, especially when he said he wanted to know everything about me.

The way he slid his thumb over my bottom lip and discreetly rubbed my ass had turned me on beyond belief. At that moment, I didn't care who saw or told what. I knew it was Sharae's messy ass that called Carlos, because she was good friends with his cousin. That was why she was watching me so hard. I'd always thought she wanted Carlos. Well, she could have his ass now. I wanted to text and tell her that shit, but I decided against that.

After my shower, I walked in the room and heard my phone chiming. I ran to it, and it said, *A'ight, girl. I'm in bed. It was good to see you tonight and I hope I can see you again, soon.*

*It was great seeing and talking to you, too. Maybe we can see each other next weekend.*

*Can I call you, so I can hear that sexy ass voice?*

Smiling slightly, I texted him back. *Please do.*

# CHAPTER 10

## STORM

I could've kicked my own ass for running my mouth like a female. On the ride home, I had time to sober up some and remember the events of the night. I let Aspen take my fucking manhood. She was slick with it too. But I didn't know what I expected from a journalist. She had the gift of gab. I even told her about Amber. *How the fuck did she do that?* Despite all that, she'd gotten what it took most women forever to get: my sensitive side. Now that she'd gotten it, how was I gon' take that shit back? Did I even want to take it back?

After my shower, I called her because she had a nigga feeling all soft and shit. Her voice was so soothing it seemed to calm everything about me. But what really had me feeling like this was that she'd broken up with her fiancé. When she told me that, I knew I wouldn't have to work as hard. She was single as fuck, and that was why she'd let her hair down some at the club. As the phone rang, I was hoping she hadn't fallen asleep yet. By the third ring, she answered. "Hello?"

She sounded groggy as hell. "Hey, beautiful. You fell asleep on me?"

"Yeah. I'm sorry. I wasn't feeling too great."

"That's all that Patrón catching up wit'cho ass."

"Tell me about it."

"That's why you shoulda came home with me."

"If I woulda went home wit'chu, I woulda ended up doing shit I wasn't ready for."

"Oh, you ready. You just don't know that shit yet. I'm gon' help you know by next weekend, though. Get some sleep. Call me whenever you have time."

"Okay. Goodnight, Storm."

"Goodnight, Aspen."

I ended the call and stroked my dick. It didn't make sense what her voice did to me. Whenever I heard it, this nigga got ready for action. My shit was throbbing 'cause he'd been hard for most of the night. To relieve myself without the mess, I went stood over the toilet and closed my eyes, allowing her voice to infiltrate my mind and my fantasies. When I did that, it didn't take my nut long to shoot out of me and into the toilet. That shit made my knees buckle. Imagining what the inside of her walls felt like was gon' have a nigga fiending for some shit he never had.

---

"WE GON' HAVE TO PUT SOME CAMERAS OUT HERE. I DON'T KNOW how, but we will."

"I know, Daddy. Maybe we can go across the street and ask Mr. Blanchard if we can install them around his place so it won't be so obvious. We can have the cameras directed to our property."

"Maybe so."

My dad and I were out in the pasture with a couple of vets, working cattle, which was giving them vitamins, trimming hooves, putting identifying ear tags, and other minor shit. We'd been out in this heat all morning, and I was tired as fuck. I'd only gotten about three hours of sleep. When my daddy called me this morning, I was mad as hell at myself. Had I remembered we had to do this

66

shit, me and Jasper would have waited until tonight to turn up. I wasn't gon' complain, though.

I got on my horse and helped round up the next round of cattle as my phone rang. Hitting the button on my Bluetooth, I answered, "Hello?"

"Good morning, Storm."

"Damn. Good morning. You sound sexy as hell."

I was fully distracted now. Not being able to focus on the damn cattle, a couple got by me. Turning around, I went rounded them back up. "I just woke up. What are you doing?"

"Working cattle. I've been up since six."

"Shit. You couldn't have gotten much sleep."

"About three hours, if that. But after this shit, I'm gon' pass out."

My phone line beeped to let me know I had an incoming call, but I didn't have time to pull my phone out my pocket to see who it was. After rounding up the stragglers and getting them to the pin, Aspen said, "We talked a lot last night, and I was kind of shocked with the conversation. Maybe we can talk more after your nap. You sound really busy."

"I am, but we are on our last round of cattle. I'll call you back on my way home."

"Okay."

I ended the call as my daddy watched me with a slight smile on his lips. He didn't say a word, but he must've heard my tenderness with Aspen. Well, he obviously didn't know it was Aspen, but he definitely knew it was a woman. I dismounted my horse and helped the vets move this shit along. I gave a couple of penicillin shots and trimmed the hooves of one. Getting home to sleep was my main objective. Then I wanted to try to talk Aspen into coming see me.

Once the day was done, I could barely keep my eyes open. After shaking hands with the veterinarians and my dad, I got in the truck and soaked up some cool air. When I pulled my phone out my pocket, I saw a missed call from Nikki. Maaaaaan, as bad as I could use some good pussy, I had to focus my energy on Aspen. She was who I wanted, so I didn't return Nikki's call. Instead, I called Aspen. Her voice was just so damned smooth, like Lalah Hathaway and shit. I couldn't stand no squeaky ass voice.

Her phone rang and when her voicemail picked up, I ended the call. She may have been busy. I knew she still had the article to write about the dying livestock around here. Things had been quiet this weekend, so it made me believe we were being watched. I called Mr. Blanchard, since Aspen didn't answer, and he gave me the okay to install the surveillance cameras around his property if I agreed to focus one of them on his property as well. He told me that he could tell someone had been in his shop. Nothing was missing, but things were somewhat scattered and out of place.

This shit was getting unnerving to me. Somebody didn't value their fucking life. Before I could get home, Dre's ass had the nerve to call me. I almost didn't answer, but I was curious as to what he would be calling me for. "Yeah," I answered.

"I have your $200. If I bring it today, can you get me a new oil pan ordered?"

"Everything is prepay for you now, nigga. If you want the oil pan, you gon' have to pay for it first."

"Man, say. We family."

"Muthafucka, family ain't shit. Family ain't paying my bills and shit. Y'all muthafuckas prolly don't even pray for me. Wishing for my downfall and shit ass niggas."

"It's like that, Storm?"

"Hell, yeah. Run me my money."

I ended the call as I turned in my driveway and entered my gate code. That bitch had nerve. Whenever he needed something, shit was about family. I didn't hear from his ass any other time. Fuck family and anybody else that didn't like it. My mama tried to get me to do more for them leaches a couple of years back, but I wasn't bending on that shit. It wasn't my job to take care of grown people. Shit, I practically did shit for free with the discounts I was giving them already. Dre was the last one that would benefit from that shit, with his broke ass.

I went inside and went straight to the shower. I smelled like I did the night I slept my ass out there with them damn cows. As much as I enjoyed taking care of our animals, I didn't wanna smell like 'em. The hot water seemed to put electrolytes back into my body, because I was drained. It didn't help that it was damn near a hundred degrees outside. The minute I stepped out my truck, I was sweating.

When I got out the shower and had dried off, I put some drawers on and laid my ass in the bed and was preparing to go to sleep when my phone chimed. It was a text message, so I checked it to see a message from Aspen. *Sorry I missed your call. I was writing and I just have quite a bit going on right now. I'll call you as soon as I can. Enjoy your nap.*

I only responded with, *A'ight.* Truthfully, I didn't have the energy to say more. After setting the phone on the nightstand and plugging it to the charger, I laid on the cool pillow and exhaled, thankful for the way my slobber was about to fuck this pillow up.

---

I WOKE UP TO THE RINGING OF MY PHONE. KNOWING THAT I'D gotten four hours of sleep, I was satisfied. I'd put my phone on 'Do Not Disturb' for four hours to assure no one would call and wake me up. Although I still felt tired, I knew I had to get up to make it to Tiffany's Washateria to get my laundry. Grabbing the phone from the nightstand, I was hoping it was Aspen, but it was this chick I used to hit months ago. "Hello?"

"Hey, Storm. It's Taneka. Did I call at a bad time?"

I frowned. This Storm chaser was never this damn considerate and proper. The ones that didn't seem to have much of a life were Storm chasers. This chick used to blow my fucking phone up. I had to block her ass for a while. The difference between them and Nikki was that Nikki was cool with what we had going on. We could go weeks without hearing from each other. After rolling my eyes, I replied, "Naw. What's up?"

"Well, I was just thinking about you. I know I fucked up the last time, and I just wanted to ask if you would be willing to give me another shot."

"Naw. I'm good on that, lil mama. Be easy."

I ended the call before she could say more. I'd be stupid as hell to start shit with her again. Getting up from the bed, I got dressed so I could go to Tiffany's and head to the shop. My phone started ringing again as I was heading out of the door. Taneka was calling back. *Here we go.* "Hello?"

"Storm. It's Taneka again. Are you involved with someone? Did I do something to you?"

"Listen, lil mama. I'm only gonna say this shit once. You too needy. I can't stand a female to be all in my space unless I want her there. We had that problem early on, that's why I quit talking to you. Don't make me block yo' ass."

"I'm sorry, Storm. I just like you a lot."

"Well, unlike my ass. Now. I don't do Storm chasers."

I ended the call and blocked her number. Why she thought we hadn't talked in all this time? I wondered how many times her ass called while she was blocked. I got in my truck and headed to Tiffany's to go deal with Cici's crazy ass.

# CHAPTER 11

## ASPEN

Carlos was making shit a lot harder than what it had to be. The place I was supposed to be moving to fell through. The owner decided he didn't want to rent it out. That shit kicked me right back to square one. Carlos was pitching a fit because my boxes were everywhere and because I hadn't moved out yet. I didn't know what the fuck he wanted me to do. I'd found another place that I liked in Houston, but it wouldn't be ready for another month. I still hadn't told my mother that we were no longer together. Mainly because I didn't feel like having to explain why.

I'd been talking to Storm almost every day. I still hadn't seen him, and I could tell he was getting impatient with me. Our conversations had become a lot shorter. It had been two weeks since I'd seen him in the club, and I finally built up the nerve to go see him and to invite him to the gala. My mama had given me an extra ticket that was supposed to be for Carlos. However, if he wanted to go to the gala, he would have to pay for his ticket. He wasn't getting this free one.

I wanted to call Storm first, but I decided to just show up in Nome. I'd gotten my things moved into a storage facility before I left, and a lot of my clothes were in my car. I'd booked a room at

Residence Inn on Westheimer; that way, I could live in peace without looking at Carlos every day. He'd become bitter and that shit was driving me insane. I was no longer biting my tongue with him and that was throwing him for a loop.

I hadn't talked to Storm in a couple of days, and I was wondering if he'd forgotten about me. My articles were sent off to various magazines, and I was free to be wherever I wanted to be, doing whatever I wanted to do. All the days we'd talked except the day after the club, he'd initiated the contact. There was just so much going on in my world. I was having to deal with Carlos and his shit, my mother and her OCD about the gala, not to mention, I had to do a writeup for it to send to Essence. It was only a month away now.

All that compounded on me trying to move and keep in touch with Storm was a lot. But that should all be behind me for now. I was no longer living with Carlos. Although I would be going to a hotel Monday morning, I was content. Going against my original decision, I called Storm. I knew he was probably working, but it dawned on me that I could be making a blank trip if I didn't call first. Looking to see it was three, I listened to the phone ring repeatedly, then finally go to voicemail.

I left a message. "Hey, Storm. I'm sorry I've been out of pocket lately and have had a lot going on, but I wanna see you this weekend if at all possible. I'm going to head your direction and get a hotel room in Beaumont. Call me back and let me know if you feel like seeing me."

I ended the call and cranked up my music, letting Vedo take my mind to other places. His "Girls Need Love" mix almost described me to the tee. I wanted Storm so badly, but I didn't want to say so. But that was all gonna change this weekend if I could help it. Although we'd only known each other a month, my infatuation with him hadn't gone anywhere. I often thought about him while I was masturbating, imagining that my dildo was him pleasing me. Those sessions were the best I'd ever had.

When I got to Dayton, I tried to call him again, and still, there was no answer. I hoped I wouldn't be spending the whole weekend in Beaumont alone. But if I did, it was my own fault for not making time to talk to him and coming out here without knowing if he was available. I went back to my Vedo playlist and enjoyed the groove, trying not to think about Storm. That was hard as hell, though, because I really wanted to see him. I guess I knew how he felt last weekend when he almost begged me to come to Nome. I just had too much shit going on.

He'd said he could help me calm down and relax and push all that negativity out of my mind. He was just the man for the job he'd said. All I could think about was what exactly he would do to calm me down. All the things I'd imagined had me feeling a way, so I could only imagine what the real thing would feel like.

Before long, I was in Nome. I had never been to Storm's house, so I didn't know where he lived. However, his family practically owned Highway 90 in Nome. As I looked at the washateria, then the barbershop, I didn't see either of his vehicles. When I got to the shop, he wasn't there, either. I took a deep breath and kept going to Beaumont. To say I was disappointed was an understatement.

After getting checked in, I went to my room and lay across the bed. Well, this wasn't exactly how I thought this would go. Storm would call me when he had time, especially if he listened to the voicemail. We'd gotten super close through phone conversation, although he'd always try to get me to have phone sex. It was so damned tempting, but I wanted my first experience with him to be face to face. Standing from the bed, I took my shirt and pants off so they wouldn't get wrinkled, then lay back down.

---

WHEN I WOKE UP, I REALIZED MY PHONE WAS RINGING. LOOKING at the clock, I realized I'd been asleep for almost three hours. Grabbing it from the bed bedside me, I quickly answered. "Hello?"

"Are you here?"

"I'm in Beaumont."

"I was mowing the hay field, so I didn't hear the phone ring. My brother was in the air-conditioned tractor and left the hot box for me. I can't believe you actually came. I thought you was scared of me."

"Why would I be scared of you?"

"You know why. What if I told you I wanted you to come stay with me instead of staying in that hotel?"

"I'd say I was hoping you would ask."

"Well damn, girl. Check out and come back. I'm gonna go take a shower, then we can figure out what we gon' eat. I don't know if I feel like eating with googly eyes on me."

"What do you mean?"

"My mama. She's been asking about you. Her and my daddy."

I giggled. "Oh okay. Well, whatever you want to do. I'm gonna head back."

"A'ight. I can't wait to see you."

Before ending the phone call, he gave me his address. I was too excited to grab my luggage and head back to the lobby. When I got down there, the receptionist asked, "Was the room not satisfactory?"

"The room was fine. I just had a change of plans."

He nodded his head, then allowed me to only pay forty dollars since I'd laid in the bed. I was grateful I didn't have to pay for a full night since I'd only been there four hours. I happily paid what he charged me, then almost ran to my car. Once inside, I cranked up and let Vedo continue to prepare my mood for Storm. I didn't know exactly what he had in mind for me, but I knew there would be plenty of kissing, touching and holding. My body was beyond ready for that type of attention, every inch of it.

What really had me in my feelings and wanting to be in Storm's arms even more so was a conversation Carlos and his friend were having about me last night. I guess he'd thought I was asleep. Hearing him say that I should be grateful that someone wanted my big ass, felt like someone had stabbed me in my heart. While he had his faults and we were no longer together, I would have never accused him of bashing my size. That shit hurt so bad I couldn't even go off on him. I'd gone back to my room and slammed the door, just so he'd know I heard him.

I didn't have any self-esteem issues, but I did have feelings. If it had been a random person or even his friend saying that, it wouldn't have bothered me one bit. But to hear him say that, someone that was supposed to love me, was heartbreaking. It made me wonder why he was with me if he felt that way. Whatever the reason, he clearly had something more to gain besides my love and loyalty.

When I arrived in Nome at Storm's house, I was in awe. It was a beautiful two-level, brick home that was hidden from the traffic passing through the town. It was tucked away on a country road that stragglers wouldn't dare be caught on. It was how he main-tained privacy. I'd put my window down to talk into the intercom but got sidetracked looking at his beautiful property. "You just gon' sit there, gorgeous?"

Storm's voice coming through the intercom scared the shit out of me. He chuckled as he opened the gate. While I couldn't see him, I knew he could see me and my reaction. I rolled my eyes and grabbed my chest, then drove through the gate. There was a barn off to the right of the home and some kind of arena looking field to the back left. I got out of my car, still looking around. There were at least four horses to the right, near the barn and a couple of peacocks roaming around.

It was so quiet, and this was what I loved about the area the last time I was here. Walking toward the house, Storm was standing in the door, only wearing some denim shorts. *Damn, he was fine as hell.* The tats on his chest and upper arms were calling me. He licked his lips as I made my way to him in my black leggings and asymmetrical shirt. I pushed my hair from my face, that I'd gotten flat ironed this morning, and smiled at him. He smiled back. "It's about time you brought yo' fine ass back to the country."

He looked at my car for a moment and frowned. I knew he could see all my shit in there. When I left from Nome, I would be going to Residence Inn. I didn't want to have to go back to the house and face Carlos again after what I'd heard last night. "It *is* about time. How've you been?"

When I got to him, he pulled me in his arms and kissed my head. "What's all that shit in your car?"

I took in a deep breath and exhaled. Instead of waiting for an answer, he grabbed my hand and led me inside. I was only gonna give him the short version of the story. After he closed the door, he led me to the oversized sectional. This house was amazing. The ceilings in the family room had to be at least twenty feet high, and the chandelier hanging from it was massive. "Damn. I'm glad to see you. Now, tell me what's up."

"I moved all my things into a storage facility except for what's in my car. I reserved a room at Residence Inn on Westheimer until my apartment is ready."

Before he could respond, the doorbell rang. He rolled his eyes, then kissed my lips, letting it linger a bit. "Mm," he said as he pulled away. "I been needing that shit. I'll be right back."

He walked away and I looked around, admiring the rest of the house. The kitchen looked pristine like he was hardly ever in it. It was in a corner of the house with a bar separating it from the family room. The huge fireplace called my attention next. As I admired the mantle and the décor, Storm's parents and his brother Jasper walked into the family room from the foyer.

"Aspen!" his mom yelled and practically ran to me.

I giggled as I stood and fell into her outstretched arms. The men had all gone to the kitchen and looked to have bags in their hands. "Hello, Mrs. Joan! It's good to see you."

"Looks like you're just in time. We all wanted to surprise Storm with a birthday barbeque, but he said he didn't feel like coming over to our house because the sun had beat him to death today while he was mowing. So, we decided to come here."

*It's his birthday?* I turned to look at Storm. He'd never told me. Our eyes met, but he quickly looked away. "Oh! He'd never told me it was his birthday."

"Seven!" his mama scolded.

He grinned slightly as he kept moving around the kitchen. I didn't know what to think of him neglecting to tell me other than him not liking attention like that. I walked to the kitchen to see chicken, two kinds of sausage, steak, boudin, and pork chops along with rice dressing mix, green beans, and bread. They were going all out for his birthday, and I was glad I was here to celebrate with them. I walked over to him and slapped his arm playfully. "Why didn't you tell me it was your birthday?"

He shrugged his shoulders as I shook Mr. Henderson's hand and Jasper hugged me. Turning my attention back to him, I tiptoed and kissed his cheek. "Well, happy birthday, sweetheart."

"Sweetheart? Ain't nothing about that nigga sweet. Ol' sour ass nigga," Jasper added.

I giggled and Mr. Henderson chuckled as Storm pushed Jasper. The doorbell rang again, and I assumed it was more family. Mrs. Henderson went to answer it and came back with his sister I remember seeing at the shop when I had the blowout. She had a huge cake in her hands. I looked up at him. "I wish you would have told me. I feel like I showed up at a party empty-handed."

"Shiiiiid, you the highlight of the party, girl."

He pulled me close to him as everybody stared at us. I didn't even think he noticed, but everyone stopped moving. He kissed my lips, and I was in shock that he displayed his sensitivity in front of them. Although they were his family, I knew he didn't really show anyone his sensitive side.

Suddenly, he pulled away from me while Jasper smiled big as hell. "Oh shit! Storm ain't no cat five no more. This nigga done weakened significantly. Nobody gotta evacuate! He just a lil tropical storm now."

I almost died laughing, like choking and everything, as everyone else hollered with laughter. Storm couldn't help but join in as he leaned over to my ear. "You see what'chu did? I'm so happy to see you, got a nigga all soft and shit."

I giggled until he bit my earlobe. That shit made my nipples stand at attention. Storm wrapped his arms around me and began walking to the couch. "I'm the birthday nigga, so y'all can handle this. Plus, I get to bring Aspen with me."

As he gently pushed me to the couch, his brother, Kenny, walked through the door with a lady and two kids. "Birthday boy!"

"What's up, y'all?"

They went to the kitchen and the kids took off to another room. Everyone seemed really comfortable, like they gathered at his house a lot. When we sat, he pulled me close. "Now back to what we were talking about. Why are you staying in a hotel?"

"My apartment won't be ready for another month, and I wanted to get out of the house with Carlos. I couldn't move on while I was living with him."

"So, why you staying in a hotel? You don't have any family you can stay with? What about your parents?"

"They don't know that Carlos and I aren't together anymore." I dropped my head, then looked back up at him as his family was moving around his house, getting everything ready. "Can we talk about this later?"

"Yeah."

Something in me wanted to bare my soul to this man. He kissed my head and said, "I don't guess you would be comfortable staying with me. But we'll talk about it later, amongst other things."

"Other things like what, Storm?"

"Other things like making you feel like a woman is supposed to feel."

Storm gently lifted my head and kissed me softly, then held me close to him while more of his family came through the door. God, it felt so good to lay against him, but I felt awkward doing so while everyone else was working. "Let me go help with the festivities. That's the least I can do since I showed up without a gift."

"But *you* are the gift."

I smiled at him, then headed to the kitchen to help the ladies. Including Mrs. Henderson, there were six women in there, and all their eyes were on me. I almost wanted to go back to the couch with Storm. Finally, one of them asked, "Girl, what'chu did to Seven? I haven't seen him this happy in a long time."

"I don't know. It was just sudden. One day he was regular ol' jackass Storm, then he became this sweet, sensitive Storm."

"Well, I applaud you, girl, because that nigga is hard as a damn steel pipe. I'm his sister, Jenahra."

"Nice to meet you," I said as I giggled.

"And spoiled. I'm Tiffany. I met you at the shop."

"Yes, I remember."

They all cracked jokes about the man I was still trying to get to know. I watched him sit on the couch and talk to one of the guys that had come in. I didn't know what made him open up to me at the club other than the fact that he was drunk, but I was glad he did. By phone we'd established a friendship, and I liked that. He'd slowed down his pursuit of me, just *for* me. I was comfortable with him, and now that I wasn't living with Carlos anymore, I was ready to do all the nasty shit he'd talked about by phone.

# CHAPTER 12

## STORM

This fine ass woman had finally come to town. I'd put my pride aside and begged her ass to come see me last weekend. I even asked her if I could come see her. I didn't give a fuck about that nigga she was with. When I saw her missed call on my phone, I got a little excited. In a short amount of time, I'd learned that she was a thinker, always planning shit out in her mind. Everything had its own timing. So, I stopped pressuring her, giving her time to get shit together.

I knew she was feeling me. If she wasn't gon' be with that nigga she was engaged to, then she was gon' be with me. From our talks on the phone, her admiration of me grew. For her to know how close I was to my family made her happy. She said that was a must in a relationship for her. So, knowing how important family was to her made me wonder why she was going to be staying in a hotel. How could her parents allow her to stay in a hotel for a whole month?

Then again, she said her parents didn't even know they'd broken up. They must've really liked him for her not to have told them by now. According to what she'd told me, she'd been unhappy with their relationship for a while. Despite all the questions I had, when I called her back and she said she was in town, I could've driven that tractor all the way home, blasting "Old Town Road".

I'd never told her about my birthday, because I didn't want her to come to town just for that. I wasn't that type of nigga that really had to have all that attention and shit. Aspen coming because she wanted to come was enough for me. That was what I wanted. I didn't have to pressure her. She came to town, because she'd finally gotten her personal shit straight, and she wanted to come and find me so she could calm the Storm looming over Nome, Texas.

When she walked up to me and I got to hold her in my arms, that shit felt unreal. The fact that I even wanted to hold her was tripping me out. When I saw her in the club, I was drunk. In my book, that emotional shit didn't count. However, this time I was sober and tired as hell, but I was still excited to see her and didn't mind showing her how excited I was. That was why everybody was shocked to see how soft and easy going I was with her. Hell, I was shocked, too.

As she talked and laughed with the ladies in the kitchen, my boy Zay had come over to chill out and to talk about using my arena to practice with Red. Them niggas was into all that rodeo shit. I didn't have time for it with the shop and everything, but my daddy had leased some steers for a few of the local rodeos. My sister was also barrel racing. Zay and Red team roped, and they knew I kept a couple of steers at my place. Red was in the process of rebuilding the arena at his place, but it wasn't ready yet.

I winked at Aspen, then Zay and I went outside to kick it with my peeps. They had the meat on the pit, and I was ready to bite into a steak, like ASAP. When we walked out, all the attention was on me. I already knew they were tripping over Aspen. "So, sis-in-law moving in?" Jasper asked jokingly.

"Naw, nosy ass nigga. She's in the process of moving. She came to see me before she got settled in."

Zay's eyes widened. "That chick in the kitchen is yo' lady?"

"I ain't tryna jinx myself and shit, but she might be soon."

"That's what's up, nigga. It's about time," Zayson said. "I wanted to ask you to be in my wedding, too, by the way."

"Shiiiid, nigga, you know I will. What's your lady's name? She from around here?"

"Kortlynn. She's from Beaumont. Legend Semien is her cousin."

"Oh okay. When's the wedding?"

"March."

We continued to talk more and clown around with my brothers and my dad. As much as I was enjoying their company, I couldn't wait until they all left so I could have Aspen all to myself. The way they were all cackling and shit in the kitchen, I knew they were talking about me. They wanted to call me spoiled, but they were the ones that had done that shit. Being the youngest of seven kids, they all looked out for me when they could. I didn't want for shit. WJ and Jenahra were grown as hell by the time I got to high school. They both had daughters and Jen was married.

When the ladies were done, they joined us outside and we enjoyed the food and festivities. I'd turned the music on, and we played Pitty Pat for money. Jasper and Tiffany accused each other of cheating as usual, and WJ and his wife tried to team up on everybody, when they knew damn well we weren't playing teams. I had to show Aspen how to play, because she'd never even seen anybody play. Bougie ass.

By the time everybody left, it was almost eleven. We'd sat outside so long, I was gonna need another shower. The minute I closed the door, I pulled Aspen in my arms and kissed her like I'd been dying to do since the minute I saw her. I didn't want to over-whelm her when she'd just gotten here. If she wasn't comfortable by now, then something was terribly wrong. I stooped and picked her up as she giggled. "Storm! Don't drop me! Shit!"

I laughed because her screams were funny. She was serious as hell. Just 'cause she was a big girl didn't mean I couldn't handle all she had to give. "I ain't gon' drop you, girl. Quit all that screaming. You can scream my name like that in a lil bit."

I carried her up the stairs while she stared at me. After this shower, I was gon' wear this shit out. But if she kept looking at me like she was, I was gon' get a taste before the shower. Aspen gently rubbed my ears, then kissed my lips. "Baby girl, listen. I wanna shower, and I'm sure you do, too, but if you keep touching me like that, you not gon' get a fresh version of me."

She died laughing as I set her on her feet. She looked around while I went to the bathroom to start the shower. I came back to the room, because I forgot we hadn't gotten any of her things from her car. However, the sight before me made me lose my whole train of thought. Aspen was getting undressed. "Aspen, what'chu doing?"

She looked confused for a moment, then somewhat embarrassed. "I thought…"

"You thought it was okay for you to unwrap my birthday gift for me? That shit just rude as hell."

She blushed, then giggled as I made my way to her. Grabbing a handful of her ass, I kissed her like she would be the last woman I kissed. When I released her, I asked, "So, what made you ready for this?"

"I've been ready. My circumstances weren't ready. I didn't want to divide my attention. You have all my attention now."

"Well, shit. Is that right?"

"Yes. I have to admit, I'm a lil nervous, though."

"Don't be. I'll take it easy on you this time. Damn, girl, you fine as fuck." I slid my fingertips down her arm, watching the goosebumps that appeared in their wake. "Where are your keys, so I can get your luggage?"

Her eyes were closed, and she moaned softly. "On the bar top."

"I'll be right back, sexy."

I left the room and practically ran downstairs. I didn't want her nerves to fester, causing her to back out of what was about to go down. That pussy been running from me for a whole month, and it was gon' lose a life tonight. When I got to her car, I kind of glanced at everything inside. Carlos was a fuck nigga that, I had a feeling, I was gon' have to check. I got her luggage from the trunk and quickly made my way back inside and up the stairs.

Damn, I wish she would just stay here. I was gon' be making trips to H-Town for sure now. Once I dug up in her shit, I knew that would be it. When I got to the room, she was sitting in the bed, waiting for me to return. I licked my lips, looking at all that ass as she stood from the bed. "Thank you, Storm. I really enjoyed your family today. Everybody was so friendly."

"You're welcome. So, umm..." Damn. Suddenly my fucking mouth went dry. I wanted to ask her the nature of our relationship, but I got nervous. *Shit.* I ain't never asked nobody that. I didn't want to expect a relationship in the long run only to find out we were just fucking. "I need to ask you something," I said in a low voice.

She stood in front of me in her bra and panties, and I wanted to just say fuck it all and take her down, especially when she rubbed her hands down my chest and grabbed the waistband of my shorts. "Let me know what'chu expect outta me."

She stared at me for a moment, then said, "I expect whatever you want to freely give. As long as I'm seeing you, I won't be seeing anyone else."

I pulled my shirt over my head and dropped my shorts. Aspen's eyes traveled south, but I quickly spun her around to free those big ass titties. I nearly salivated at the sight of them. Her nipples were hard as I ran my hands over them. Listening to her moans were about to make this storm catastrophic. My dick was straining to break free of my boxer briefs, and I wasn't about to let him suffer any longer. Stepping back from her, she turned to me to watch me reveal the monster in the Storm. When I freed him, her eyes stayed fixed on him as she licked her lips. Like she was in a trance.

I walked closer to her, then gently pulled down her underwear. It seemed as if she stopped breathing, and I could feel her body tremble. "Let's go shower, before we don't."

She walked over to her bag and bent over to get something out of it and shit, I almost lost it when I saw that shit between her legs. *Fuck!* It was just as fat as I thought it was. "Shit, Aspen. You did that shit on purpose. Let me get my ass to this bathroom before I fuck the shit out of you."

I grabbed my dick as she blushed, holding her shower gel in her hand. I walked away to the bathroom, then yelled, "Get'cho ass in here, Aspen!"

As I opened the shower door, she joined me in the bathroom. Just at the sight of her, my dick throbbed. He could smell pussy, and he was ready to dive in it. As she walked into the shower, I wanted to slap her ass, but I kept my hands to myself, for now. When I joined her, she immediately pulled me to her and kissed me. I backed her to the wall and let my hands roam her body. Pulling away from her, I lowered my mouth to those melons on her chest.

My hand eased between her legs and when I felt how juicy her shit was, I couldn't help but moan in response. "Damn, baby. Yo' shit juicy as hell. Is it always like this?" I mumbled in her ear.

"Every time you touch it, it will be."

I kissed her neck while I finger fucked her slow. She moaned and said softly, "Stooorm, yeeesss."

She was so close to cumming it was killing her. I could tell she was holding it by the way her body was trembling, and her muscles were clenched. Instead of questioning her, I just continued to enjoy being close to her and enjoying the feel of her wet pussy, gently stroking that g-spot. Her legs were trembling more and if she held it in any longer, her ass was gon' hit that floor. I began lapping at her nipples again and when I firmly sucked one, she finally bust. The way she screamed and grabbed my head was so damn sexy.

I continued to stroke her until she was clawing my back up. This was that freaky shit I'd been missing in my life. Freaks these days wanted to be as strong as me, like sex was a fucking competition on who could get who to bend in submission first. That was that stupid shit. Aspen was letting me know that I'd pleased her, and I loved that shit. I didn't stop stroking until she came again.

She was so drunk with passion, it looked like she would fall over any minute. "Let me wash you, baby girl."

I soaped her loofah with her Olay Shea Butter body wash, then began passing it over her body as she moaned. This shit was new to me. I had never taken a shower with a chick before. Most times it was straight fucking, then somebody was leaving depending on the location. Amber and I had never taken a shower together, either. We were both usually so busy trying to get our business straight, we rarely took time to just appreciate each other. The great thing about Aspen and me was that we were both established in our careers to where we could breathe.

Continuing to wash her body was only making my dick leak. She looked embarrassed when I lifted the roll of skin on her side to wash underneath it. Aspen closed her eyes for a moment. "What just happened, baby girl? You look like something bothering you."

"It's nothing."

"Naw, we ain't finna start lying to each other. We've been pretty open for the past couple of weeks. What's up?"

"I've just been having a hard time getting Carlos' words out of my head. I overheard him tell his friend last night that my big ass should've been grateful somebody wanted me."

I knew I didn't like that fucker. He was gon' get fucked up, on some real shit. She continued, "I'm used to random people saying hateful shit to me or about me, but to hear him say it made me question his motives. It made me feel like our whole relationship had been a lie."

"Well, check this. I desire every part of your body, and I'm gon' show you that shit when we get out this shower. He a bitch nigga that don't know perfection when it's staring him in the face. You perfect as hell. You hear me?"

"Yeah. I'm not doubting myself. You don't have to worry about that. I know I'm fly as shit, but it hurt to hear those words coming from his lips."

"Fuck him. He not worth your energy."

She smiled slightly at me, then wrapped her arms around me as

I washed her back. Once I was done washing her, I quickly washed myself, then we got out. She was trying to wash me, too, but I wasn't feeling that shit. I wasn't trying to feel that sensitive. We got out of the shower and dried off, then I led Aspen to the bed. She lay in it and exhaled loudly. "Damn, your bed is so comfortable."

"Mmm. Wait 'til you feel the owner."

# CHAPTER 13

## ASPEN

S torm got in bed with me, and I thought my body was gonna automatically combust. He was moving so slowly with me. It felt like he was torturing my ass. I completely expected him to fuck me in the shower, but he was being so cautious of how I would respond to him. I rolled over and looked at him. "Storm, I just want you to know that just because I'm nervous, it doesn't mean that I will regret being with you. I haven't slept with another man in over four years. Carlos has been the only one during that time. That's what my nerves are about. So, quit being this weak ass Storm that don't know if it wanna make landfall."

His eyebrows shot up. "What the fuck you said to me? You been around Jasper's ass too much today. Weak ass storm, huh? So, you want catastrophic damage."

He reached over and dug in his nightstand. I got on my knees and slurped his shit up. That dick was so beautiful. Not a blemish in sight. It had just the right amount of girth, and it was as long as I thought it would be from looking at his dick print. Storm grabbed my hair and pulled me off it. He was holding my hair tightly as he looked at me. While licking his lips, he slowly lowered me back to his dick.

He was so fucking sexy. I'd be his private concubine for the rest of my life. As I began pleasing him with my mouth, he thrusted and damn near made me throw up. I should have let weak ass Storm hang around in the Gulf, because I had a feeling he was gonna have me calling on Jesus in just a minute. I adjusted to his thrusts as the tears fell from my eyes and let him fuck my mouth. The grip he had on my hair let me know he was in full control, and I'd given him that with my slick ass mouth.

I did my best to suck the hell out of it while he thrusted and evidently, I was doing just that because he whispered, "Fuck, Aspen!"

That only propelled me forward, sucking harder, moaning as I did so, like his dick was a delicious ass popsicle that I couldn't get enough of. Storm was so manly, in every sense of the word, but he was gonna give in to me tonight, whether he wanted to or not. His control was crumbling as I wore his dick out with my best work. He'd stopped thrusting as hard and was enjoying what I was doing to him. My hair was free of his grasp, but he now had his palm on the side of my face, his fingers threaded through my hair.

When I looked up at him, his stare was on me, and it was one of passion, desire, and admiration of my skills. He'd underestimated my sexual prowess. But I was putting him on notice, and he didn't know how to handle that from me, his lil bougie baby, as he'd called me jokingly in one of our phone conversations. I continued to stare at him, watching him bite his bottom lip. He hadn't made much sound, but I knew he was fighting it. His facial expressions and body language were saying it all. They were saying, *please baby don't stop* and *suck the fuck out of your dick.*

And my dick it was. Everything in his demeanor was submitting to the power I was stripping from him as I indulged from root to tip. His dick was down my damn throat, but I'd gotten in the right position to be able to take almost all of him, and he seemed overwhelmed by it all. "Aspen, shit. I'm about to nut."

I gazed up at him again and continued to suck but increased my pace. Storm grabbed my hair with both hands and began thrusting into my mouth as he released. His grunts were so damn sexy. I allowed his nut to leave my mouth as I continued to suck his dick. It was a lot. Sometimes I swallowed, but I wanted to be his freak tonight, letting him see how much I liked the taste of his shit. He grunted loudly as I stared at him. Then he scared the shit of me when he yelled, "Fuck!"

He pushed me off him, then grabbed the condom he'd sat on his nightstand and strapped up quicker than I'd ever seen. Storm pulled me up, then pushed me to my stomach and filled me up. "Oh, fuck!"

I couldn't help but scream that out. Storm remained still for a moment, and I could hear a soft grunt leave his lips. It was like he was finally home, the place he'd craved his whole life and that grunt was the relief in knowing he'd finally found it. Grabbing my ass, he began a slow but hard rhythm as his dick made promises of fucking up everything it touched. My cervix was awakened and had me trying to scoot away from him. "Naw, baby girl. You said to quit being a weak ass Storm. So you gotta take all this dick."

I closed my eyes and bit the pillow as he leaned over, hovering over me as he plunged his dick in my pussy, shocking every nerve in there. This orgasm was about to be massive, and my body was already becoming overwhelmed by what hadn't even happened yet. I was trembling everywhere, not just my legs, and it was even evident in my voice. "Stooorm, fuck! You disrupting shit!"

"Then I must need to go harder. I wanna destroy shit… ruining you for anybody but me. Now sink this muthafucka."

He bit my shoulder as he fucked me hard and grabbed my hair, pulling my head back. My orgasm submitted to his demands, and I screamed loudly as it left me, draining me of control. I basked in the feeling it washed over my body as he punished me for making him wait. Moving his hand from my hair to my neck, he squeezed, pulling my head backwards. "Stooorrm!"

My voice was somewhat restricted due to his grip on me, but just that had me about to cum again. He kissed my neck, then bit my earlobe and grunted in my ear. He was about to cum, but he was trying to hold it. I lifted my hips and began to twerk on his ass. His stroke stuttered for a second, then he popped the fuck out of my ass. That shit stung for real, and I knew his handprint would be there for days. I continued to ride his ass as he stroked me, trying to pull that nut from him. Grunts continued to come from him as he stroked. Sliding his hand under me, he grabbed my nipple, causing me to cum instantly.

Storm's strokes became more powerful and faster as I felt my body trembling, giving him everything he wanted from me. His thrusts were almost unbearable, but I took it and lifted my hips, allowing him deeper access. "Fuck!"

He'd gotten the nut my shit was trying to pull from him upon his entry, but I was surprised that I didn't feel its deflation. He pulled out of me as he panted, then got out of bed without a word. I turned over to see him enter the bathroom, then come back out with a wet towel. There was a smirk on his lips. "That shit was as good as I imagined. As you can see, I ain't done with you."

He handed the towel to me and continued. "You're bleeding a lil bit, so this next round I'm about to give you something nobody has ever gotten. I hope you ready."

*I was bleeding?* My eyes had to have widened as I sat up and stood to my feet, inspecting the bed. There was no blood on his bed. It wasn't time for my period, so I was nervous as hell. He could obviously tell that I was losing it a bit. "Aspen, calm down, baby girl. That just means you hadn't been getting fucked properly. All that shit finna change now, though. My dick and your cervix about to get real acquainted."

He walked over to me and grabbed the towel from me, gently wiping my prized possession with the same tenderness he'd shown me in the shower. As he did, my phone started ringing. A part of me wanted to answer it or at least see who it was calling me this late, but the rational part of me didn't want to disrupt the atmosphere Storm had taken his time to set. Ignoring the phone, I pulled him to me and kissed his lips. That call would have to wait.

"WHERE ARE YOU, ASPEN? WHY DIDN'T YOU ANSWER MY CALL last night?"

"Mom, it was after midnight. I was out," I lied as Storm smirked and pulled me in his arms.

We'd fucked all night into the morning. The last thing I wanted to do was argue with my mama. All I wanted to concentrate on was how good I felt. Storm had done my body right. Once he saw how flexible I was, he had my body in positions I'd only dreamed about. The minute I bounced on his dick, I knew he was addicted to my ass. I was addicted to him, too. The way his dick rocked my ass to sleep was something I would never get enough of.

With Carlos, I could do all kinds of shit after sex. I'd get up, take a shower, wash my hair and shit, and have full pampering sessions. But shit. After Storm, all I was fit to do was go to sleep. I didn't even remember falling asleep last night, but when I woke up in his arms, I was beyond happy to be there. I snuggled up to him and had gone back to sleep until my phone rang at nine this morning. "Where are you, Aspen? Carlos said you left and didn't tell him where you were going."

I couldn't believe his ass had called my mama, trying to make it look like I was the bad person. "Mom, Carlos and I broke up two weeks ago. So, I don't know why he's putting on that he's so worried about the big girl who should have been grateful that he even wanted me."

"What? Why didn't you tell me? Where are you staying?"

"I know how you feel about Carlos, and I wasn't ready to face your disappointment. I moved out yesterday, and I'll be staying at Residence Inn until my apartment is ready."

"Aspen. You're my daughter. I know I tried to convince you to accept Carlos's way of doing things, but the decision is yours. I'll still be in your corner no matter what. I love you, baby."

My heart turned to mush as Storm kissed my head and got out of bed. "I love you, too, Mommy."

93

"So, what happened? I mean, besides what you guys were already in disagreement on. Did Carlos say that about you?"

"I fell out of love with Carlos a while ago. We just weren't a great match. He's a good person, just not the one for me. And yes, I overheard him saying that to someone else over the phone."

"I'm sorry, Aspen. Would you like to meet me for lunch so we can discuss your living arrangement? I know you like your independence and privacy, but one of our properties is vacant. Maybe you can stay there rent free."

"I'm out of town. I'll be back Monday. Maybe we can have lunch on Tuesday."

"Where are you?"

"I'm in Nome, Texas, where I'd come a month ago to do a writeup."

"Okay. Well… umm… That's fine. I have to go, so I'll call you after this meeting."

"Okay. Bye."

I took a deep breath, because I knew her wheels were turning when I told her where I was. There was no reason for me to be here unless I was working. So, I was sure she knew a man was involved. I got out of bed to brush my teeth. Storm had started the shower. "Good morning, baby girl."

"Good morning," I replied as I walked into his embrace.

"How did the rest of the conversation go?"

"It went okay. My mom kind of shies away from confrontation, so when I told her where I was, she found a way to get off the phone. Speaking of, would you be interested in going to a gala with me next month?"

"A gala?"

"Yeah. My parents are putting it on to raise money for Alzheimer's research."

"Umm… if you want me there, I'll be there. I'm not really used to attending formal events."

"Well, get your tuxedo ready, Storm. You think you can handle that?"

"I can handle whatever, especially if I'm gon' be wit'cho fine ass."

Storm gently popped my ass while I walked to the vanity. After grabbing my toothbrush and I began brushing, I couldn't get over how happy I felt about being here with him. This just felt so right. Or maybe it was the excitement of being with someone as rough and different as he was. I'd never been exposed to a rude ass nigga like him that could be as sensitive and caring as he was at times.

I was attracted to him from the beginning, like a pill popper to Percocet, but that night in the club really changed my perception of him. He gave me a sneak peek of what all he had to offer. I thought his rude side was pulling me in, but it was what I couldn't see that attracted me to him. His rude side turned me on, but his sensitivity was what brought me back.

When I was done, I went back to Storm's room to get dressed with a smile on my lips. This was so new and refreshing, I couldn't contain my excitement.

# CHAPTER 14

## STORM

"Where you feel like eating? We can go to Beaumont and get something, then chill out a lil bit or shop. Whatever you wanna do."

"Okay. Can we get some seafood?"

"Yeah. Whatever you want."

I was tired as fuck, but I couldn't get enough of this woman. When she slurped my shit up, I wanted to scream like a bitch. That shit was so good, I could barely contain myself. But when I dove in her, it was like she sucked me in, literally and figuratively. At that moment, I wanted to be everything she wanted a nigga to be. So, if she wanted me at this gala, I'd be there in my tuxedo, with her on my arm.

After getting dressed, we took off for Beaumont with my sights set on Team Gilliam's. If she wanted seafood, their seafood boil on Saturdays was the best thing going. There was shrimp, sausage, potato, corn, boiled egg and a huge snow crab. That egg boiled in that seasoning was everything. We made small talk on the way to Beaumont about the gala and about her plans for the writeup she had to do for it. We also talked about my shop and how I needed to hire another mechanic. I had to close the mechanic bay of the shop because my employee had a family emergency. Normally, I would have gone in, but wasn't no way I was going in with baby girl here.

When we got to Gilliam's on Eleventh Street, I helped Aspen out the truck, and we went inside. I swallowed hard when we walked in because Nikki was standing there, looking to be waiting on her order. She smiled until she realized I was with Aspen. I assumed she'd thought I'd just opened the door for her until Aspen waited for me. I grabbed her hand to send a silent message to Nikki. Unfortunately, she didn't catch the hint because she walked right on over.

"Hey, Storm. What's up?"

"What's up, Nikki?"

"Not too much. What'chu been up to?" she asked, glancing at Aspen. "I haven't seen you in almost two months."

"Stop being rude as fuck, Nikki. Aspen has been keeping me busy. Usually, when a nigga stop talking to you, it's because he's lost interest. Now, get the fuck out my face before I embarrass you."

Aspen's eyebrows had risen while Nikki frowned. "Oh, so that's what we on, Storm?"

"Yeah, because yo' ass was being messy and disrespectful when you brought yo' ass over here. This my queen. That's the only time I'm gon' explain that shit."

*Shit.* More of my thoughts had come out than I planned. "Damn. I was just being cordial, Storm. But I apologize if you thought I was being shady. I apologize Miss."

Aspen nodded at Nikki's fake ass attempt at innocence. She forgot that although we were just fucking at one time, that I knew her ass. She was the queen of petty. I'd witnessed her doing this shit to another nigga. That was how I met her ass. She'd seen me watching and gave me the eye while I'd licked my lips. I was ignorant to the whole situation back then, but I was almost sure that she was doing the exact same thing. When she walked away, I looked over at Aspen and she looked uncomfortable. "I'm sorry, baby girl. I'll explain later."

She nodded, and we walked to the counter to order our seafood platters. I could see her glancing at me. When we stepped to the side, the older guy behind us reached out to shake my hand. I frowned slightly, trying to figure out if I knew him. He said, "Naw. We don't know each other." He must've seen the confusion on my face. "That's how you shut a ratchet ass female down and not let her disrespect your lady. I applaud you, youngster."

I nodded at him, then turned to Aspen. I grabbed her hand again. "Me and her messed around for a few months, but that was before I met you. We were never serious or no shit like that."

"I'm not tripping on that, Storm. But I'm starting to think that you want me to be yours, like right now. I'm your queen?"

"Just like you ain't gon' be fucking with nobody else, neither will I. You might as well be mine, girl," I said as I pulled her close to me. "And yeah. You a queen, baby girl. My queen. I'ma really show you tonight. I was anxious last night. You don't wanna be mine?"

"It's not that I don't want to be yours, Storm Henderson, but I just got out of a relationship. I didn't wanna hop into another one so soon. I wanna make sure I'm ready and not doing that just because I'm feeling vulnerable or lonely. But I am very interested in you."

She gently rubbed my cheek. I guess I could understand where she was coming from. Although my situation with Amber was more tragic, Aspen was the first woman I'd seriously entertained and wanted to be mine since then, and Amber had been dead for over three years now. I grabbed her hand from my face and kissed it. "I feel you, baby girl. We'll go at your pace."

She smiled at me as they called my name for our order. I went to the counter and thanked the lady, then walked back to her. When she opened that box, her eyes widened, then she looked up at me. I chuckled. She looked like one of those emojis with hearts in place of the eyes. "This is a lot of food."

"I know. And it's good, too."

We were silent for a while 'cause the food had our full attention. When we finally took the time to look at each other, we both had a mouthful and couldn't help but laugh. I was glad she didn't think too seriously about that issue with Nikki. I was surprised she'd tried me. Nikki knew how I got down and that I didn't have a problem calling out anybody on their bullshit. She wasn't the exception. Once I'd finished and Aspen had eaten as much as she could, we left. "So, where are we going now?"

"Where do you wanna go?"

"I just wanna be with you, so it doesn't matter."

"See, you can't be saying shit like that. I have no problem going back to Nome and keeping you all to myself until you leave. Although, you don't really have to leave."

"Well, let's go back to Nome. And I do have to leave."

"A'ight. We gon' make one stop, then we'll head back."

I decided not to press the issue of her staying. It would be a lost cause. I drove over to Nothing Bundt Cakes to get us some dessert for later. I could think of all kinds of shit I could do with all the icing on that cake. "You like Lemon?"

"I love Lemon."

"Perfect. Me too."

I got out of the truck to get our lemon mini bundts, and while I was in the bakery, my phone started ringing. Nikki. She was gon' make me get real ugly with her ass. Everybody knew that if you were fucking somebody and they showed up somewhere where you were, you either ignored them or spoke and kept it moving. She knew exactly what she was doing, and I wasn't for the games. I answered the phone despite all that. "Yeah?"

"You know, I thought we were better than that. I would have never thought you would have talked to me like I was some random bitch. That shit was hurtful and embarrassing."

"Nikki, I'm not one for games. You know that shit. Secondly, you a playa, so you know the fucking code. When you saw I was with someone, which I made sure you did by grabbing her hand, you should've just kept it moving. You could have sent me a text later to say whatever you wanted to say. It wasn't that I had something to hide, because you were before her, but it was disrespectful the way you tried to stand there and have a fucking conversation like she wasn't standing there. That was the shit that fucked me up, 'cause I thought you were better than that and above the ratchet shit."

She was quiet for a second. "Whatever, Storm. I'll talk to you later."

"Naw. Don't call me no more. If I want or need you, I'll call you."

I ended the call before she could respond, then blocked her number. Before long, I was gonna have more blocked numbers than accessible contacts. After retrieving my minis from the clerk, I headed back to the truck to see Aspen on her phone. I guess I wasn't the only one with shit to clear up. She had a deep frown on her face. We weren't even together yet and was having to put people in their place. When I got in the truck, Aspen said in the phone, "Mom, I will call you later."

"You okay?"

"I'm so sick of Carlos. He told my mama that I was cheating on him with you. My fucking nerves are on edge, and I want to drive to Katy and let his ass have it."

"Don't worry about that nigga. He ain't got shit else to do but act like a lil bitch. I got'chu, baby."

I grabbed her hand and kissed it after setting the box on the back seat. She exhaled, then turned to me. "My mom, the one that doesn't like confrontation actually called me and confronted me about our freak show at the club. Sharae told him and he told my mama. I can't stand drama. I should've stayed my ass home that night."

"If you wouldn't have come, we wouldn't have reconnected. Let's just get back to the house so I can help you get your mind off that shit."

She only nodded her head. I could see the anger all over her and I knew the feeling. Backing out the driveway, I headed home to soothe her soul.

---

Before getting home, I had to stop by WJ's house. He had the forks to attach to the tractor bucket. I was gonna need them once Kenny bailed the hay. When we got there, WJ's wife was driving his truck through the yard with the trailer attached and their daughters were on the back, having the time of their lives. If that wasn't some country shit, I didn't know what it was. We sat there for a while, watching them and laughing. "What pleasure are they getting out of that?" Aspen asked.

"The same pleasure kids get being pulled in a wagon. The trailer is just a big ass wagon."

Aspen laughed. "I guess so."

"You wanna get out?"

"No. I'll see them later on at your parents' house, right? I need to call my mama back."

"Yeah, they'll be there. Okay, I'll be right back."

I hopped out the truck as the girls screamed, "Hi, Uncle Storm!"

I waved at them and went to the barn where WJ was working. He and his oldest daughter was in there and he looked to be showing her something. I admired him. His oldest daughter was with another woman. After she got locked up, he took his two-year-old daughter and raised her himself, teaching her things that people didn't normally teach their little girls. That girl knew how to operate a tractor and was learning how to work on them. She was so receptive to whatever he taught her. That shit was gon' put her so far ahead of the game.

WJ waved me over. I didn't want to interrupt whatever they were doing. I hugged my niece, Nesha, then shook his hand. "Oh, my bad. I forgot you were coming to get the forks."

"Yep."

"Aspen still in town?"

"Yeah. She's in the truck talking to her mama."

"I must say, I'm completely shocked. This came so out of the blue. I didn't know you were feeling her."

"Yeah. Jasper knew. I think Mama and Daddy had an idea. I don't know what it was, but the minute I saw her, I knew I had to have her."

He turned and looked at me. "Have her sexually or the real deal?"

"Well, at first it was sexual, but after she opened her mouth, it became more. I put my shit on the table, but I was a lil too rough with her. Scared her ass right out of Nome. She left the same day."

WJ laughed, and I joined him. I could laugh about the shit now, but I was in my feelings when it happened. He grabbed the attachment and handed it to me. We shook hands again and agreed to see each other later. I kissed Nesha then walked out to go to the truck. I waved at the girls and WJ's wife, then put the fork attachment in the bed of the truck. After getting in the truck with Aspen, I noticed she looked like she'd been crying, but she looked over at me and smiled. I smiled back. "I have some vanilla ice cream at home to go with our minis."

"Sounds good," she said, doing her best to sound happy.

"You okay?"

"Yes. I'll be better when I can lay in your arms."

"Shiiiiid, me too."

She giggled as I left my brother's driveway and wondered what the hell her mama had to say about me.

# CHAPTER 15

## ASPEN

S torm and I had had an amazing time while I was there. It had been three weeks since then, and it was the weekend of the gala. Storm was still coming, despite my mama telling me not to bring him. I'd told her if Storm couldn't come, then I wasn't coming, either. Carlos was going to be there with his parents, and she said it would be a slap in his face for me to show up with Storm. *Fuck Carlos!* Of course, I didn't say that to her, but I sure in the hell wanted to.

Storm had come to visit me weekend before last, and I'd driven to Nome last weekend. I'd spent a lot of time with his family, because he had inventory to do at his shop. Being with him was the best decision I'd ever made. Storm was so passionate and loving, things I never would have taken him for in the beginning. We talked every day, and we'd gotten so close. It was strange how we connected. After I'd left to go to the hotel from my first visit, I knew that he would be the one.

We'd fucked in every way imaginable and every weekend after that, Storm showed me some different shit that he could make my body do. I was so damn turned on I'd squirted for the first time. Something that I noticed as well was that during sex, my mind didn't wander to other things going on in my life. Storm had my undivided attention. The way his dick spoke to my body was a language only he and I could understand. He made me feel powerful and made me submit all at the same damn time. He'd become a little more vocal during sex as well.

The last time I'd come to Nome had been different though. Despite the fact that he was at the shop the whole day Saturday, when he'd come home, he told me he was gonna make love to me. That shit was so mind-blowing, I had to lay in the bed for a while to remember my own fucking name. He was so tender it almost didn't seem like the same man. He'd said it was his gift to me and I knew without a shadow of a doubt that I was all his. I planned to tell him that tonight.

As I got dressed in my black wrap dress, there was a knock at my hotel room door. I only had one more week to be here, then I could move into my apartment. I couldn't be happier about that shit. I walked to the door and peeped out to see Storm. When I opened it, he had to be a smart ass. "What'chu peeping for? You was expecting somebody else?"

"You never know in a hotel."

Swiftly pulling me to him with one arm as he held his tux in the air with the other, he nibbled on my earlobe. "Hey. I missed you, baby."

"Hey, baby. I missed you too."

When he lifted his head, I kissed his lips. Every weekend, we did the same thing. It was like we were torturing ourselves being away from one another. More like me torturing us. It was my decision to stay apart. It was my decision to not fully give in to him. Technically, I had, but not with the title. Tonight, when we came back to make love, I would tell him, and I couldn't wait to see his face when I did. "Let me go start on my makeup. I know you don't like all that shit, but I have to wear something. We'll probably be on TV, too."

"I'm not tripping on that, girl. Do your thang. I'll get dressed while you do that. I didn't want to get all wrinkle on the drive over."

I nodded, then went to the bathroom to do my makeup. I didn't know what I was thinking by putting this dress on first, so I took it off, then proceeded to go through my metamorphosis.

After I'd done my makeup and my hair, I put my dress back on, along with my heels and walked out to see a very debonair nigga named Seven Storm Henderson. He was in all black, and I could've stayed in this hotel and devoured every bit of him. "Damn!"

"A nigga clean up nice, huh?"

"Hell yeah."

"You look sexy as fuck, girl. I hope I can keep my hands to myself tonight."

I giggled as he approached me and kissed my neck. I was just praying things went well. Against my mother's wishes, I hadn't brought Storm to meet them, and when I told her he owned a mechanic shop in Nome, she almost lost her cool. She didn't even let me finish explaining how well-rounded and smart Storm was. Nor did she know that he came from a family of prestige and wealth. She and Daddy heard mechanic shop, and that was it. They thought he was some random guy that saw I had a flat tire. Even if he was, nothing would be wrong with that.

When we got to the gala, my anxiety kicked up a notch. I didn't want anyone to cause a scene, because Storm wouldn't hesitate to rain and blow category five force winds all over this gala. However, I couldn't have him going to jail over no foolishness. I honestly didn't think he would take it that far, but I wasn't sure how he would handle being provoked. "Damn. Welcome to bougie-ville."

I giggled a little as Storm looked around at all the people in attendance. My brother immediately came over and hugged and kissed me, then shook Storm's hand as his camera hung around his neck. "Storm, this is my brother, Dallas."

"Nice meeting you," Dallas said.

Storm nodded. I knew Dallas was waiting on a further description of who Storm was in my life, but he wasn't getting it. I didn't want to say he was my friend, because he was so much more than that. He was my confidant when I needed to talk.

He was my lover that took care of my body like no man ever had.

He was my mechanic when my lil Optima wanted to throw shade.

He was my partner in life without the papers.

Storm had quickly infiltrated every aspect of my life, and I wasn't angry about it. He kept me mentally stimulated and entertained at the same time. He even helped me with my introduction for the writeup on the gala. My brother turned back to me and looked me over. "You look really nice, sis."

"Thanks, Dallas. So do you."

"Well, let me get a picture of the two of you before your mother finds me to ask why I'm not taking pictures."

I smiled, then stood close to Storm. He put his arm around me, and I circled mine around his waist and lay my other on his chest. Dallas briefly peeked around his camera and looked at us, then went back to take the picture. "Y'all look amazing together. I had to look at y'all again, away from the lens."

I glanced at Storm as he smiled. "Thanks, man."

He and Dallas shook hands again and had some form of silent communication, because they nodded at each other. I didn't know what that meant, so the minute Dallas walked away, I was sure to ask. "What was that look and nod y'all gave each other?"

"It was like a take care of my sister look. So, I nodded. I plan to take care of you so well, you won't remember hurtful times. You'll only remember the bliss you in from being with me."

I looked up at him, clearly at a loss for words. There wasn't any profanity or sexually charged words in what he said. Nor was there any slang. My hand eased up to his face, and I ran my fingers through his beard. He pulled my hand from his beard and kissed it, then led me to our seats. I was so lost in him I never saw my mother approaching. "Hello, Aspen."

I lifted my eyes away from Storm to meet hers. "Hi, Mom."

Storm immediately stood and turned to her to greet her. "Mom, this is Storm Henderson. Storm, this is my mother, Celeste St. Andrews."

"Hello, Mrs. St. Andrews. It's nice to meet you."

She nodded her head and extended her hand to shake his. "It's nice meeting you as well, Mr. Henderson. Do enjoy tonight."

He nodded, then said, "Yes, ma'am."

She leaned in to kiss my cheek, then said softly in my ear, "We need to talk."

I didn't respond to her verbally. As Storm and I sat, he smiled at me. "She seemed nice."

"Most times, she is."

I closed my eyes briefly and opened them to see Storm watching me. Revealing to him what my parents really thought about him had never crossed my mind until now. I didn't want him to be blindsided if something popped off. While my mother would be cordial and hide her true feelings, my daddy was just the opposite. He wouldn't verbally insult Storm, but he *would* remain silent, pretending that Storm wasn't even standing there. That was what made me nervous. I didn't know how Storm would react to that. I wouldn't have to wait long, because I saw my mom tell him something, causing him to look over at us with a frown on his face. Could have sworn I was a kid.

He made his way over and I said to Storm, "Here he comes. Don't let him bother you."

Storm glanced over his shoulder, then back at me. His face had reddened a little bit, and I could tell the wall went up. When my daddy approached us, Storm stood to his feet out of respect as I hugged my daddy. "Hey, baby girl. You look beautiful."

"Thanks. Daddy, this is Storm Henderson. Storm, this is my father, Joshua St. Andrews."

Storm held his hand out to shake my daddy's hand. He looked

at Storm's hand for a moment, then back up at his face, then shook his hand as I exhaled. "Nice to meet you, Mr. St. Andrews."

"Likewise."

I slowly released the breath I was holding from my mouth. Daddy turned to me and smiled. "Talk to you after the gala."

He winked at me, then walked away. As we sat, Storm said, "I thought that was gon' be bad for a minute."

"Me too. I'm sure Dallas was somewhere taking pictures of the whole exchange."

Storm chuckled as the band started to play and the lights dimmed. I leaned in closer to him and he draped his arm around me. This felt like home, and I knew it was where I belonged. Once the band had finished their number, my parents appeared at the podium. I picked up my cell phone from the table to record and that was when I saw him. Carlos. Slightly rolling my eyes, I sank deeper into Storm's embrace as he glanced at me.

He was so attentive to me and could always tell when something was bothering me. As my parents talked, the lights had come back up and Carlos's eyes had fallen on me. I could see them shift from me to Storm, then back to me. Storm had to have noticed, too, because he pulled me even closer. If we were any closer, I'd be in his lap.

Storm's grip on me had tightened as well. He probably didn't want to say anything since I was recording. Storm had never seen Carlos before, but with the way Carlos was staring, he had to assume that was who he was.

When my parents finished talking and everyone applauded, the staff began serving dinner. "I assume that's your ex."

Storm's face was a little redder, so I turned his face to me and stared in his eyes. "Yeah, but what does that have to do with us?"

He smiled slightly. "Not a muthafucking thang."

He leaned in and kissed my lips. That was such a damn tease. It was like my body went up in flames. Being so close to him and then him kissing me, did things to my body that I couldn't even explain. We stared at one another, and my breathing pattern changed completely. I wanted to leave this damn gala now, and it had barely gotten started good. Storm leaned into me, talking directly in my ear. "Baby, if I didn't know any better, I would think you were imagining that you were bouncing on this big dick."

My nipples had gotten so hard, and my clit was tingling in my thong. If I moved just right, I knew I would cum all over myself. I wanted to give him my tongue so badly it was killing me. It felt like I was miles away and didn't hear or see a thing that was going on, except for what was right next to me. "You should know better, baby. That's all I can think about with the way you're looking at me, with your sexy ass."

He smirked at me and asked, "You tryna make me hard, huh? All these lil old white ladies gon' pass out when they see this dick print. That's what you want?"

"I just want the dick, daddy. I can't wait to leave."

"We ain't gotta leave. I'll give it to you in a bathroom stall if you want it that bad. Ain't no shame in what I put down."

I seriously thought about that shit for a minute while he laughed. *God, what was he doing to me?* Thankfully, the servers had set our dinner plates in front of us. The smell of that steak brought me all the way back, and I wasn't the only one. Storm sat straight up. I looked at him and giggled. "Foreplay on hold. This shit smell good."

I sat up, too, and we began eating. The steak was so good, my eyes closed as I chewed. Along with that was asparagus, some kind of potatoes and a dinner roll. We also had a side salad and glasses of wine, water and tea. My parents had done an excellent job planning this event, and I was anxious to see who they'd gotten to perform. The generic tickets she'd given me didn't say who the special guest would be.

As I ate, I'd occasionally look up and see Carlos staring at me. I was hoping Storm was too consumed with his food to notice. "I have to be honest. I ate on my way to Houston because I didn't know how the food would taste."

I laughed. "So you were prepared."

"Hell yeah. I couldn't be sitting here hungry, girl."

I laughed again as I finished up my dinner. Unlike him, I hadn't eaten since breakfast, so I was starving. As I pat the corners of my mouth, that shit went dry when I saw Carlos approaching our table. Hopefully, I didn't have to embarrass him the way Storm had embarrassed ol' girl when we'd gone to get something to eat a while ago. Storm put his fork down and glanced at me. Neither of us stood when he approached, but he had three magazines in his hands. "Hello, Aspen. These came in the mail for you."

I realized they were the farm magazines I'd submitted my story, too. There was also a couple of envelopes between the magazines. "Hello, Carlos. Thank you."

Storm's eyes never left Carlos's, and I knew if we hadn't been in the environment we were in, Carlos wouldn't have been safe. Carlos was still standing there, and I wasn't sure why, so I looked up at him. "Is there something else?"

He looked around, then said, "Actually, there is. Can I speak to you in private?"

I frowned and looked at Storm to find his eyes on me. Those eyes were saying, *You can get yo' ass up if you want to, but I'ma snatch yo' ass back down.* I calmly looked back at Carlos. "No, you can't. There's nothing further we need to discuss. I'm no longer in the house with you, we weren't married, and we don't have children. So, what more could we have to talk about?"

The people sitting near us were starting to stare at us, and I could see Carlos's embarrassment in his demeanor. "So, I guess you're letting his culture rub off on you."

Storm stood before I could stop him. I stood along with him. Carlos smirked and walked away. He was such a jackass. As we both sat, I said, "I'm sorry, Storm."

"You don't have to apologize for that jackass, but he better not come back over here."

I held onto his arm as I noticed Dallas watching us with a frown on his face. Ignoring the eyes around the table, I turned Storm's face to mine by putting my hand to his cheek. I didn't say a word, just stared into his angry eyes. I watched them eventually ease and when he was calm, he did what he always did. He pulled my hand from his face and kissed it. "Thank you, baby."

Storm began to feed me some cake, and we seductively stared at one another while we ate. Not long before we finished our dessert, my mom went back to the podium to introduce Gladys Knight. I couldn't have been happier. I'd always loved Gladys Knight. "My mama would be in hog heaven right now. She loves this woman. So much so, I think she would probably leave my daddy for a shot at Gladys."

I laughed as his face lit up with excitement. "I should have gotten her and Daddy tickets."

He began taking pictures with his phone as she started to sing "Neither One of Us". That was one of my favorite songs by her. As she sang, Carlos's eyes kept darting back to me. He was gonna make Storm fuck him up. Why he thought he was better than Storm was beyond me. Storm could run circles around his ass as far as money was concerned. He just didn't flaunt it, and I loved that about him. He had a nice house and two vehicles. They weren't top of the line in extravagance, but they were affordable for anyone with a decent job.

As Gladys continued to her next song, Storm leaned over and kissed my cheek. Then I realized that Carlos was fucking with him because he thought he was soft. Storm was only soft with me, and Carlos had that shit twisted. If I didn't think one of these officers would arrest Storm, I would let him beat the fuck out of Carlos. People were starting to get up and dance, and what I saw next put my nerves on edge. Carlos had stood from his seat and was walking toward us. "I don't wanna embarrass you, Aspen, but I will put him in his place."

"I know. I just don't want things to get out of hand and you end up handcuffed."

"I'm not worried about no cuffs, but I am worried about him thinking that I'm beneath him. He gon' get the shit he looking for."

I took a deep breath, hoping that Carlos would walk past us as I held on to Storm's arm. As luck would have it, he stopped in front of our table again. Luck was never on my fucking side. I could see Dallas taking picture after picture, the camera pointed right at us. *Shit! Shit! Shit!* "Aspen, would you like to dance?"

Before I could answer him, Storm said, "If you don't carry yo' disrespectful ass on, you gon' be dancing yo' bitch ass to Methodist Hospital. Keep fucking with me and mine and find out how I get down. I don't give a fuck about who watching."

I tightened my grip on Storm's arm, trying to calm him down, but it seemed I was nonexistent to him at the moment. His face was red as the flames of hell. Carlos smirked, then turned to look at Gladys as she started the next song. "So, umm… Aspen as independent as you are, you're letting someone else speak for you?"

"I've already told you to leave me the fuck alone, but clearly you didn't get that memo. A real man protects what's his, not talk about them behind their backs."

Even with me holding on to Storm, he stood and knocked the fuck out of Carlos. I flopped down in the chair and covered my face momentarily to hide my disappointment and embarrassment. Carlos was out for the count, and a couple of officers came over and escorted Storm away from the table. I walked out with them, and my brother met us in the foyer as well. The embarrassment on my parents' faces would be something I would remember and something they would never let me forget.

Since Storm willingly left the gala, the officers allowed him to explain. Then they got me to corroborate his story. Dallas quickly added that he had pictures and video footage of Carlos approaching our table. Once they'd seen it, Dallas went back inside to continue taking pictures. I was so glad we were seated near the back to where what happened didn't disturb the concert.

Storm looked at me and nodded toward the door as my parents approached. They both appeared angry. The officers were going to allow us to re-enter the gala and keep Carlos out, but my daddy said, "Arrest this thug. You can't go around punching people because you don't like them."

Storm frowned. "No disrespect, Mr. St. Andrews, but name calling ain't allowed. I haven't disrespected you, and I would damn well appreciate if you didn't disrespect me."

"You disrespected me the minute you decided to act like an animal at our fundraising event. Get him the hell out of here."

"Daddy! So defending my honor is unforgiveable?"

"Aspen, we will talk to you later. In the meantime, you have a job to do. I expect you back inside."

I looked over at Storm, and he had a scowl on his face as my parents walked away. I lowered my head and exhaled loudly. "Go on back inside. I can see you embarrassed about this shit. I'm sure you'll have a ride back to your hotel. It seem like you having a hard time choosing between the thug that give a fuck about you and your ignorant ass parents. I don't have time for the dramatics and bullshit."

With that he walked off. *What in the fuck just happened?* "Storm!" I yelled and ran after him. "I get that you're pissed, but I'm not one of them, so you don't get to talk to me like that. I'm not supposed to get overwhelmed with the situation? I can't take a fucking minute to take a deep breath?"

"But I bet you're going back inside. That shit should be a no brainer, but here you are thinking about which decision you gon' make. Don't lie to me and say you weren't thinking about that shit. I'm used to not being a priority."

"I'm not your ex."

"Apparently, you aren't my current, either. I'm going all out for a chick, willing to go to jail and shit, that won't even acknowledge me as her man. I'm out."

I was so in shock I didn't know what to do with myself. I stood there and watched him walk to his Range. That shit hurt. As I turned to go back inside, I saw Carlos walking out. He looked like he wanted to say something to me, so I ducked off into the restroom. I couldn't deal with his bullshit, or I might slap the fuck out of him. This shit was unbelievable. Reaching into my clutch, I called Storm, but he didn't answer. He jumped to all sorts of conclusions.

Then I had to ask myself the question. *Would I have left with him before his blowup?* Yeah, because he meant everything to me. He didn't give me a chance to choose. It wasn't like I depended on my parents for anything. He was the one that had helped me through my issues with Carlos. I never expected Carlos to be so stupid. I was thinking my parents would have been the problem. Leaving the bathroom, I looked around to make sure Carlos was gone, then headed inside to get my shit off the table.

Gladys was taking a break and a doctor was at the podium talking about the effects Alzheimer's has on the body. I snatched my magazines and other mail from the table and went back out into the foyer to call for an uber. As soon as I walked out, I ran into Carlos. "Get the fuck away from me!"

"Aspen, let me explain. I love you, and it's hard for me to just sit there and watch you try to pursue something with someone else. Can we try this again?"

"No! Leave me alone!"

"You heard my sister. Now get the fuck away from her before yo' ass get knocked out again."

I turned to see Dallas approaching. Carlos raised his hands in surrender and went back inside the gala. Everything in me wanted to cry, but I couldn't. It was partially my fault. Although Storm had said for me to take my time, me not giving him a title had clearly bothered him. I felt like had I acknowledged us as a couple, things would have gone differently. Dallas put his arm around me as I called for an Uber. After giving my address and ending the call, he looked down at me. "You okay?"

I shook my head, trying to keep the tears at bay. He pulled me in his arms and hugged me tightly. My younger brother had only held me like this one other time, and that was from a heartbreak when I was in high school. He kissed my head. "How long for your Uber?"

"Fifteen minutes."

"That was pretty quick."

"Yeah."

I leaned against the wall, wishing tonight was all a nightmare. Fuck the writeup, fuck Carlos, and even fuck Storm. I guess I was about to get the time I should've taken to be alone without letting a man complicate shit.

# CHAPTER 16

## STORM

I threw my keys on the countertop and went to the fridge and got a beer. Tonight was a disaster, and I didn't make the shit any better. The only thing about tonight that I regretted was that I exploded on Aspen. I didn't give her a chance, and that was my bad. It was like I thought about Amber and how she'd chosen getting her paper over me. *I'm not your ex.*

Aspen had clearly seen what that was about. She was nothing like Amber. She'd called a couple of times, but I couldn't bring myself to answer the phone. I was still pissed with the way her daddy had spoken to me, not to mention that fuck ass nigga she used to deal with. Now that I was sitting here in my feelings, I was ready to talk about my blowup and apologize to her. Grabbing my phone from my pocket, I called her back, hoping that she would answer.

I left her there to fend for herself, when she'd gotten there with me. My behavior was embarrassing to her. As I sat listening to her voicemail, I let her voice soothe my soul, then left a message. "I'm sorry, baby. I was tripping. Please forgive me."

I ended the call and hoped like hell she would call me back. So, when my phone started ringing, I just knew it was her, but it wasn't. It was Jasper. "What's up, nigga?"

"Get'cho ass to Grayburg right now. Them muthafuckas out here. One on a fucking horse roping shit and another one doing something with the feed look like."

"Shit. I'll be there in a few minutes. Call the police."

I didn't bother taking off my tuxedo. Bolting out the door, I got in my truck and burnt off. If I pushed it hard enough, I could be there in less than five minutes. That was just what I did. When I got there, the noise from my truck alerted them. They started running to their vehicle, leaving the damn horse they were roping cattle from in the pasture. They didn't get to it before I could raise my gun, though. My hunting rifle was in my truck, but I'd also brought my .38. When I got closer, I noticed a familiar face. Jasper had gotten out of his truck and had a gun pulled, too.

I noticed he had a female with him. He was probably on his way home and saw their asses from afar. "What the fuck y'all fucking with our shit for?" I asked the white guy.

He refused to answer. When the black guy got closer, I realized we'd gone to school together. "Man, what the fuck you on? You know this shit is a federal offense?"

"I'm on the same shit yo' punk ass daddy on."

Before I knew it, I'd put my gun to his head. "What the fuck you said?"

As he was about to speak, the police had arrived and pulled their guns on me. "Storm! Put that gun down! We got it from here."

Because we were in a small town and our family was as affluent as we were, everybody knew us, but even as under the radar as I tried to stay, the cops knew me whether I wanted them to or not. "Say what you were about to say," I said to the guy.

"Wesley Henderson is my daddy. But he didn't give a damn about taking care of his responsibility 'cause he didn't wanna look bad in the community."

I was stunned into silence for a second. I lowered my gun and looked over at Jasper to see if he heard this shit I was hearing. He looked just as stunned as I did. "Who's your mama?"

"Cici."

"What the fuck? You a lying ass nigga. Cici is a family friend."

"Whatever. She said Wesley is my daddy. He been giving her a lil hush money, but that's it. That nigga didn't think I wanted him to be in my life like he was in y'all's life? Fuck you if you don't believe that shit."

One of the cops had eased up on me and said, "Come on, Storm. We need you to back off, man. We got it."

I walked away and put my hunting rifle back in my truck as they arrested the two guys, then I saw Jasper and a cop running after somebody else. They must have been hiding under the shed where I slept at that night. I could see Jasper dive on somebody like he was wrestling a damn steer, then I heard him scream and a gunshot.

I immediately ran to them because the cop was on his walkie asking for a bust. My heart was about to beat out of my chest. If Jasper was shot, I was gon' take out them other two. When I got close, I saw that Jasper was holding his leg, but Cici lay next to him, dead.

"Man, this shit is fucked up. You a'ight, Jasper?"

"Nigga, I been stabbed. Naw I ain't a'ight!"

I rolled my eyes, then got on my knees to look at Cici. Realizing she wasn't dead yet, I said to her, "How could you do this to my mama? Y'all were friends."

She couldn't answer me because she was struggling to breathe. She started gurgling, and I knew she was about to die. I hated that shit. Cici was so damn cool, but to know my daddy fucked her only fueled my anger. An ambulance arrived, and they ran out to the pasture to get Cici and Jasper. When her son saw her, he started screaming. This shit was fucked all the way up. They were killing cattle because they were angry with Daddy. I pulled my phone from my pocket and called him. "Hello?"

"Get'cho ass to Grayburg. Now."

"Storm?"

"Wesley. Now."

I ended the call. I'd never spoken to my dad that way, but my anger was consuming me. Although I tried to keep that shit contained, because they could have been lying, I couldn't help it. The look in his eyes when he said that shit told me that he was serious as hell. Wesley was gon' explain some shit to me. My mama was walking around, thinking he was the perfect husband, and he was fucking with one of her classmates. Then the bitch had the nerve to be working for Tiffany and flirting with me. The shit was about to hit the fan, and I was gon' make sure that fan was on full speed. It was gon' be a whole shit storm.

They loaded Jasper in the ambulance and said they were taking him to Baptist Hospital in Beaumont. I called Tiffany and she said she would meet them there. As I ended the call, I could see my daddy arriving. I had to pace, because I wanted to go over there and fuck him up for fucking over our mama. And not just fucking over her, but him having evidence of the shit was what was blowing me. He got out of his truck with a frown on his face. One police car was still there, making a report I assumed. Two cars had gone to the station with the guys they arrested, and another had gone to the hospital.

That nigga was two years under me in school, and he was my fucking brother. The police officer got out of his car and walked over to Daddy before he could get to me, so that stalled the inevitable. As I paced back and forth, my phone was ringing. I looked at it to see Aspen's number. I quickly answered. "Hello?"

"Hey."

"Hey."

"I got your message."

I remained quiet to see what else she would say. My daddy was walking toward me with a frown on his face. Oh, but he was gonna wipe that shit off in a minute. "I really am sorry, Aspen."

"I know, Storm. I'm sorry, too. I'm on my way down, because I want you to look at the article in the magazines."

"I think we figured it out. But I'll tell you about it when you get here. I got somebody I gotta talk to."

"Okay. I'll see you in about an hour."

"A'ight."

I ended the call, then stared my old man in the face. My face was twitching, and I wanted to knock his old ass out. He stared at me like he was aggravated. "Storm, I don't appreciate the way you spoke to me over the phone. What has gotten into you to where you feel like that was okay?"

"Any secrets you keeping from the family? If not, I'll apologize. If so, then you deserve everything that's swirling around inside of me."

He looked at the ground and back at me. It seemed he got a little nervous. His ass should be nervous, because I was gonna tell all my siblings. Jasper got stabbed over this shit. That alone could have been so much worse. His secret could have killed Jasper. That thought made me wanna snatch him up. "Seven, I know it looks bad…"

"You don't have that privilege anymore. It's Storm to you."

"It looks bad because we kept it from y'all."

"What do you mean, we?"

"Your mama knows about this."

"It not only looks bad, old man, it *is* bad. I went to school with a brother I ain't even know about. You fucked somebody else and created an everyday reminder of your infidelity."

"Storm! That's enough! You will respect me!"

"Like you respected Mama when you fucked Cici? I'm out. I gotta check on my brother who could have died over this bullshit."

I walked away from him as he stood there in shock. I could tell he was pissed, but he could be pissed all day as long as he wasn't near me. Once I was in my truck, I peeled out, anger consuming me. I'd been angry most of the night and I just wanted to be, but Aspen was coming in the midst of all this bullshit. Running my hands down my face, I tried to focus my thoughts on Jasper, so I called Tiffany. "Hello?"

"You made it there yet?"

"Yes. They've taken him into surgery. The doctor said he'd lost a lot of blood, so they had to do something immediately. She could have hit a major artery. Was it a large knife?"

"Yeah. I'm on my way."

"You okay, Seven?"

"Not really, but eventually, I will be. We'll talk when I get there."

"Okay. He said he wasn't sure how long they would be in surgery because they weren't sure of the extent of the damage yet, but he would update us as they progressed."

"Okay. See you in a lil bit."

As I drove, I rationalized tonight's events in my head. The Storm was weakening, and I was starting to feel hurt and sensitive. A lot of shit had gone down tonight, and my resolve was crumbling. First, I'd had to knock out Aspen's ex and defend myself against her parents. Then I snapped on her, possibly killing the future I wanted with her. I was falling for her, and the shit was unnerving because I didn't think she felt the same. Then to get here and learn of all the shit that had gone on in the past without my knowledge was overwhelming.

The man I'd always looked up to had fallen off the pedestal I had him on. Sure, everybody fucked up from time to time, but I'd never expected him to fuck up in that way. He'd always told me when I chose the right woman, that my loyalty to her and only her would be one of the most important aspects of our relationship. So to know he wasn't loyal to the woman he'd been married to now for over forty years did something to me. It made him seem like a hypocrite.

Everything I aspired to be in my life was because of my admiration of him and my older brother, WJ. Everywhere they went, I went and everything they did, I wanted to do. That was why when things went wrong when it came to the animals, everyone called me. It was my dad's love for animals that had inspired me to love them, too. I used to also help him work on tractors and change tires. Everything I'd become was because of mainly his influence. To know he'd fathered a kid and didn't even offer him a chance to be influenced by him because of how it looked to other people pissed me off.

When I got to the hospital, I messaged Tiffany to see where she was. She informed me she was on the second floor, so I got out of my truck and headed that way. Before I got inside, I called Aspen to tell her where to find the spare key. "Hello?"

"Hey. How close are you?"

"Umm... about twenty minutes away."

"I'm not there, but there's a key under the mat and you remember the gate code, right?"

"I remember, Storm. What's going on?"

"I'm at the hospital. Jasper got stabbed, and he's in surgery."

"Stabbed?"

"Yeah."

I proceeded to tell her about tonight's events, and she was completely silent while I explained. She wanted to come to the hospital to meet me. I let her know that I wasn't in the best mood and being at the hospital was only pissing me off even more. She giggled when I said that, and I couldn't understand what was so funny, until she said, "You're acting like I haven't seen you angry or experienced you being a jackass."

I chuckled for a second, then realized it would benefit me to have her here. "A'ight."

I gave her directions, then walked inside and up the stairs to see Tiffany, WJ, and Kenny. My other two sisters were probably in route, and I was pretty sure my parents would be here in a little while as well. I sat next to WJ with a frown on my face. "What happened out there?"

I looked at the three of them and asked, "Who's gonna retell this story to Jenahra and Chrissy? Because I'm not repeating it when they get here."

No one said a word, so I sat back in my seat, prepared to keep my mouth shut. Finally, WJ spoke up. "I'll tell them."

I sat up once again. "Jasper called me because the people that had been fucking with our cattle were out there. When I got there, they saw me and were trying to leave, so I pulled my rifle. We were standing waiting on the police and when they got there, Jasper and one of the cops saw somebody moving by the feed. They chased them down and when Jasper dove on her, she stabbed him."

"Her?"

"Yeah. Here's the fucked up part. It was Cici. One of the guys that was injecting cattle is her son. Guess who his daddy is?"

Looking around at their confused faces, I also saw Mama and Daddy getting off the elevator. I nodded my head in their direction and said, "He just got his ass off the elevator and is heading this way."

"Where's Cici? Her ass better be in jail. Working at my damn washateria, like she best friends with the family," Tiffany said.

"She dead, Tiff. When she stabbed Jasper, the cop shot her. Had he not, she probably would have killed Jasper. Fuck, she could have killed him with the first swing of that knife. Thank God it was his leg and not his chest or something. Other than that, Wesley's lil secret and neglectful ass actions would have gotten our brother killed," I said as he walked up.

The four of us were all scowling at him. I knew he'd heard my last statement, because his frown mirrored ours. "How's Jasper?" he asked.

Tiffany was the only one that wanted to speak up to answer him. "We don't know yet. He's in surgery, and he lost a lot of blood."

He nodded his head as Mama sat next to Tiffany. "I know you're all upset and disappointed in my actions. All I can say is that I'm sorry. I apologized to your mother years ago, and she chose to forgive me. I pray y'all choose to do the same."

With that, he sat next to Mama on the other side of Tiffany as

Jenahra and Chrissy arrived, with Aspen in tow. I stood to my feet and exhaled at the sight of her beauty. Instead of letting her greet the family, I grabbed her hand and walked away. It might have been selfish, but I didn't give a fuck right now. She was mine, and I was going to benefit from her soothing spirit before anyone else could.

# CHAPTER 17

## ASPEN

Before I could speak to anyone, Storm had whisked me away and brought me back downstairs. Tonight had been rough on him, clearly by his actions and the scowl on his face. I didn't know how I would react to knowing my daddy had a secret love child. Anger would for sure be one of the emotions I would be feeling. I didn't know what I would say to calm him down, but I hated to see him so angry. Beyond that anger was hurt. While I knew he didn't want me to see it, I could see the little boy that looked up to his daddy through his eyes.

He brought me to a secluded area of the ER, and we sat down. He hugged me and kissed my cheek. "I'm sorry for how I snapped on you earlier. I didn't really give you a chance to make a choice. Even more so, I shouldn't have gotten angry, because you aren't mine, regardless of how much I want you to be. It's just that... I feel some shit for you that I can't seem to control and it's making me crazy. I know you don't feel the same way, so I'm tryna chill out, but I can't. I can't resist the urge to call you mine. I can't stop being possessive and shit. And most importantly... I can't believe I'm about to say this shit, but I can't stop myself from falling for you."

My eyes were wide, and my heart had turned to mush. This man said he was falling for me. I couldn't let him reveal the secrets of his heart and not tell him what I knew to be true. Although, I'd wanted to tell him while we were making love tonight, I knew I couldn't stay silent after this. I lifted my hands to his face, and I wanted to kiss him, but I refrained. I gently rubbed my thumbs across his cheeks as my other fingers sat in his beard. "Storm, I *am* yours."

I let my hands drop as he stared at me in disbelief. His lips parted, then closed again. I smiled, then kissed his lips. "Aspen. You saying a nigga got you on lock?"

I giggled. "Well, lock means marriage in my book, but umm… I'm saying you're the only man I want. Storm Henderson is the only man I need."

"Seven."

"Huh?"

"Aspen, you've proven to be loyal. And since you are special to me and I'm obviously special to you, you're free to call me Seven. Whenever you want."

"Well, damn. I done been deemed worthy and shit!"

Storm's eyebrows rose and he laughed, then pulled me from my seat. He hugged me tightly, then kissed my head and led me back toward the waiting area on the second floor. Grabbing my hand, he smiled. "I never expected you to say that. I just wanted to let you know how I felt and shit."

"I've felt it for a couple of weeks or so. I wanted to be sure. I'd planned to tell you after the gala while we were making love, but I didn't expect things to go the way they did."

He lowered his head for a second as I continued. "I expected you to do what you did in response. I didn't expect Carlos to approach us."

"Man, you just don't know how sensitive you got a nigga, now."

He chuckled but that quickly came to a halt when he saw the doctor talking to his family. We quickly ran to them to hear the doctor saying they had to give Jasper blood and how they had to repair a nicked vein in his leg. He was gonna have to go through rehab, but ultimately, he would be fine and make a full recovery. Once he left, I greeted everyone. Storm's two sisters that I came in with didn't seem to be too happy now. Everyone seemed to have a permanent frown on their faces. They probably didn't know about the secret son when we'd arrived.

I was going to have to retract my story from the magazines. Those were only the preliminary copies for me to read over that they'd sent. The thought of someone trying to get back at his dad was the furthest thing from my mind. However, I didn't want people to start sniffing around Nome and find out their personal business. I had the perfect story to put in place of it. I stepped away from the family and made the necessary phone calls. Of course, I would have to return the checks. I informed them that they hadn't been cashed, so I would return the original checks.

When I rejoined the family, there was a full-fledged argument going on between Mr. Henderson and Storm. I quickly got between them, along with Mrs. Henderson. Storm's brothers were all trying to pull him away, but when I stood there, pleading with my eyes, he grabbed my hand and yanked me away. I rubbed his arm and said softly, "This isn't the place for this, Storm."

"Tiff, call me when they move Jasper to a private room."

We went to the elevator and went down. "Fuck!" he whispered roughly.

I held on to his arm, rubbing it with my other hand, trying to soothe him. I knew how he was feeling somewhat, since I'd gotten into it with my parents before I left. They'd criticized everything about him, including his name, calling him a thug and saying how disrespectful he was. I yelled at them, telling them that Storm wasn't the one at fault here. Carlos was the one that fucked up our night. We were at our table minding our business. Then they tried to say that we ruined the gala with our theatrics and wanted me to give them ten grand.

I nearly lost it on the phone with them. They complained that people left the event when Storm hit Carlos, so we cost them money. Not to mention how I didn't stay at the gala, which meant I wouldn't be able to provide the writeup I promised, since I wasn't there. I was so outdone with their accusations I told them fine. I would borrow the money from Storm, since his family practically owned the whole town. That shut them the fuck up. Their assumptions about him rubbed me raw. It wasn't that I didn't have the money, but I wanted to shut them up about Storm.

I couldn't understand why they were calling him a thug anyway. None of his tattoos were visible, because the tuxedo had covered it. Even if he had worn a short-sleeved shirt, they still wouldn't have been able to see them. His tattoos didn't pass his elbow, and none were on his neck. The only thing I could see they were judging him for were his diamond earrings and the way he spoke. He had a slight country twang, mixed with an urban dialect, but tonight, he'd been on it. He spoke proper English except when he talked to Carlos.

So, it looked like we were both on bad terms with our families. He and his dad could somehow mend their relationship once he cooled off. But my relationship? I didn't know. It seemed it was all about the amount of money they thought Storm lacked. Our relationship had nothing to do with money, and their approval of our relationship should have nothing to do with money, either. Even if we resolved our differences, I would know that their attitude with Storm was fake.

When the elevator stopped, Storm led me to his Range. Once we got there, he opened the door to the backseat. I didn't question it, I just slid in. He closed the door, then walked around and started the engine and got in the back seat with me. The moment he did, he pulled my face to his and kissed me hungrily, devouring my mouth like he hadn't tasted it in years. I moaned into his mouth, because this was the exact thing I wanted to do when he said he was falling for me. As he sucked my bottom lip, I let my hands travel to caress his dick through his pants.

He moaned in my mouth, then slid his hands through my hair

and gripped it. Pulling my head back he began tongue kissing my neck and gently sucking it as he traveled south. His hands slid under my shirt, then pulled my breast from the bra and caressed my nipple. They were extra sensitive to his touch, and I could feel my clit protruding. "Stoooorm. Shit."

He slid his hand up my thigh and squeezed it. If I wasn't a big girl, I would have straddled him in this Range by now. There wasn't enough room in the back seat, though. Storm lifted my shirt, then brought his lips to my nipple. As he made love to it, by gently sucking it, I came in my panties. "Oh, fuck!"

He lifted his head and looked at me. "You came, baby?"

"Yeeessss," I moaned as I dropped my head back, its effects lingering.

Storm slid his hand in my leggings as I lifted one leg in the air. He looked up at it and smirked, then found my pearl and stroked that shit until I was cumming again. What shocked me, though, was that he brought his long, slender fingers to his mouth and sucked them clean. Storm had never eaten me out, but I felt like it was safe to assume that he would as soon as possible. He stared at me for a moment, then said, "This some good shit. Can I get another taste, baby?"

"You can have whatever the fuck you want, Seven."

"Oh yeah? Whatever the fuck I want? We gon' have some shit to talk about then, baby. I like the way Seven rolls off your lips, too."

He slid his hands back in my leggings and stroked me unselfishly, like he was about to nut from that shit. Again, pulling my nipple in his mouth, I couldn't contain how amazing just his fingers felt. After checking on Jasper, getting to his house would be my number one priority. I was so damn horny, I didn't know how I would be around everybody, knowing what his fingers had done to me, how they'd stroked me into ecstasy. Storm lifted his head and said in my ear, "I can't wait until you can bust all over my lips. You taste good as fuck. You wanna bust on my lips, baby?"

"Yeeeeesss. I can't wait."

His voice in my ear was throwing fuel on the raging fire below and when he licked my earlobe, I came so hard, I didn't know how I would get out the SUV, let alone be around his people. That shit had zapped all the energy from me. Once again, after the tremors had died down, Storm brought his fingers to his mouth and sucked them. He then brought them to my lips, and I sucked his fingers like I was sucking his dick.

The excitement and wanting coursing through his body was evident, and just as he was about to pull his dick from his tuxedo pants, his phone rang. Smirking at me, he grabbed his phone from the console and answered. "Hello...? A'ight. We on our way back in. What room...? Okay."

He ended the call and looked at me. "To be continued. Jasper's asking for me."

"Okay, baby. You and Jasper are the closest, huh?"

"Yeah. Me, him, and Tiffany. We're all within a five-year age span."

He opened the door and helped me out the back seat. Draping his arm around my shoulders, we headed to the entrance as the chick he'd gotten into it with at Gilliam's that Saturday walked out. She smirked at us but didn't say a word. I just knew there would be some shit, because Storm was already on edge. He would have given that girl the business, for real. But just as I thought that, I heard, "Storm!"

He didn't even turn around to acknowledge her, which was really big of him. But I knew he was trying to get to Jasper. This shit wouldn't be over, though. I had a feeling that once he knew Jasper was good and we were going home for the night, he was gonna call her ass. When we'd gotten inside to Jasper's room, Jasper was waiting on him. "'Bout time you get in here. Did you see if Chasity got home in my truck or not?"

"Nigga, shit. After all that, I forgot somebody was in your truck. You trust her?"

"Yeah, she good people. She probably blowing my phone up to see where I am, but I don't know where the fuck that shit at."

"You know her number by heart? I'll text her."

"Naw, I don't."

"Why the hell she didn't get out the truck when she saw you on the gurney?"

"I told her, no matter what, not to get out the truck."

"Nigga, I guess."

As I watched the two of them converse, I got a glimpse of his dad, sitting in the recliner. He looked so weary. I could only imagine how he was feeling. At least his wife already knew about it. That would have only made the situation worse if she didn't. I still couldn't understand why they wouldn't tell their kids. Kenny stood and let me sit next to Tiffany as Storm turned towards his daddy. I was hoping I didn't have to stand between them again. Storm seemed to be hurt the most by his infidelity and secret child. He rubbed his hand down his face. "Why did you keep it a secret?"

His dad looked up at him as his brothers got in position to handle the situation if it got out of hand again. Mr. Henderson looked so hurt to be in the position with Storm that he was in. "I had a huge deal with the Douget's going down. I couldn't ruin my opportunity to gain almost everything I have now with scandal. I took care of him and Cici financially, but I wasn't a father to him and never had a relationship with him. I regret that every day of my life."

The tear slid down his daddy's face, and he quickly wiped it. Storm didn't say a word in response. He turned his head back to Jasper, and they began discussing what the doctor had said and how long he would be in the hospital. To see Storm and his daddy's bond severed was heartbreaking, but I knew they would eventually repair what was broken, rebuild what was torn down, and carefully maintain what had been neglected.

# CHAPTER 18

## STORM

O n the way home, my daddy consumed my thoughts. While his reasoning for what he did wasn't acceptable, I could understand. Trying to maintain peace amongst his children, the seven of us, was what had concerned him. Keeping his son a secret was one thing, but the fact that he neglected him too was what brought all this shit on. When I saw the tear slide down his face, it softened me some. I'd never seen my dad cry. I'd gotten that toughness from him. Crying showed weakness and Henderson men weren't weak. I don't remember ever seeing any of my brothers cry, either.

My thoughts were running through my mind at the speed of light. I hadn't said much to Aspen all the way home, but she'd sat there quietly, leaving me to my thoughts while she rubbed my hand between hers. As I turned in the driveway, I turned to her and asked, "How long you plan on staying, baby?"

"I don't know. I have another story to write."

I frowned at her. She had better not be talking about this shit. After all the inner feelings I'd given her ass, I'd damn near kill her ass if she fucked me over. "What kind of story?"

"Well, I retracted the first one because I didn't want anyone coming down here looking for answers and digging in shit they have no business in. So, I think I'm gonna do a story on you."

I frowned even harder. Being in the spotlight wasn't my thing, which was why a lot of people around town didn't know my connection to the family. Since I was the youngest, people tended to look over me. Aspen continued. "Don't worry. I won't put your picture in it. Just a picture of your shop and talk about how you function in a small town, running a successful business."

"That shit ain't gon' sell. You gon' *have* to put a picture of all this greatness to catch people's attention."

She hollered with laughter. I'd do all kinds of shit for her, and I hoped she realized how much I cut for her already. To know she felt the same way for me eased my soul. The way she calmed me down when I was almost at the point of no return, further assured me that this shit between us was real. It was predestined or some shit. I wasn't a nigga of poetic words or nothing like that, but her aura brought that shit out of me. Had me saying stuff I couldn't have even dreamed of.

She was mine, though, and I couldn't wait to show her what being mine felt like. Nikki was vying for that spot all of a sudden, but that bitch had another thing coming. Tomorrow, when we came to visit Jasper and Aspen got her car, I was gon' call her and let her ass have it. I couldn't stand a jealous ho, especially one that thought more of herself than she should. I didn't give two fucks about Nikki. Pussy came a dime a dozen for a nigga like me, but Aspen… she was rare. She was a treasure that I stumbled on. I then realized had it not been for my daddy's fuck up, I would have never met her. So, I guess I owed him.

After helping Aspen from the SUV, I led her to the door as her phone rang. She dug in her purse and answered. I wasn't trying to listen to her conversation, but I could clearly tell she was talking to her brother. He seemed cool. While unlocking the door, shifting my thoughts to Aspen's juicy ass pussy, she said, "Dallas said what's up and that he's sorry how things went down tonight."

"He don't have shit to apologize for."

After I deactivated the alarm system, that I often questioned why I had, I went to the kitchen to pour me a drink. I could leave the gate open, and the house unlocked and didn't have to worry about nothing coming up missing or anybody traipsing around my property. I watched Aspen get the bottle of Stella Rosa from the fridge. She'd bought that the last time she was here. I either did beer or the hard shit. I wasn't a nigga that drank wine or none of that fruity shit, so that bottle had stayed right where she left it.

As I drank my Henny, she ended her call and came sat on my lap. She shouldn't have done that shit. "Either put that glass down or gulp that shit."

I gulped my Henny and sat it on the coffee table as my hand rested on her thigh. Aspen stared at me for a second as if she was wondering if I was serious or not. This hard dick should have told her just how serious I was. She gulped her wine, then sat the glass on the table next to my cup. Sliding her off my lap, I laid her on the couch right next to me. Standing to my feet, I immediately pulled off her heels, then her leggings and soaking wet thong.

I could see her body trembling as I admired it in all its glory. Her body was everything I'd always desired. It was so soft, and it craved me just as much as I craved it. Aspen sat up and pulled her shirt off, then unfastened her bra. After pulling my unbuttoned dress shirt off and taking off my wife beater, I couldn't help but lower my lips to hers. I needed to kiss her so bad, my body felt like it was going into withdrawals trying to be romantic and shit.

Kissing her slowly was threatening to fuck up my insides, but I needed to show her all the passion I held inside for her. Unfastening my dress pants, I let them fall to the floor, revealing my hard dick that had the front of my drawers wet. It had been leaking since before we got to see Jasper and that shit was pure torture. "Mm. He's ready for me, Storm."

"Uh huh. He been ready for you, but I wanna taste your pussy first."

I hadn't eaten pussy in a long ass time, since Amber and I were together. That shit was like riding a bike though. I ate so much pussy back then, I couldn't dare forget the technique. "Well, shit. Do that shit, then."

I loved when she talked dirty. The precum had leaked right out of me as she said those words and lifted her legs in the air. She was so damned flexible. I loved that shit. When we'd finally fucked for the first time and baby spread them legs like she did, I was in awe of her. The whole night, I kept her legs wide and high. Tonight would be no different. She grabbed her ankles, and I went to my knees, looking at her sloppy wetness. When my lips touched her lower ones, I knew I would never get enough.

The moan that left her, just from feeling me graze her pussy lips and breathe on her shit, caused me to dive all the way in. When I indulged, I didn't even wanna come up for air. Slurping up all her juices, I began teasing that clit in circular motions with my tongue, then sucked on it as her hands rested at the back of my head. "Storm, shit! Why you been keeping this shit to yourself?"

I moaned against her clit, then reached up and pinched her nipples. Her legs began trembling, and she started screaming out her release. My beard was soaking wet. I was doing my best not to waste a drop, but baby girl was on constant lubricate. I slid my finger in her ass and her eyes opened. She stared at me as I stroked her asshole, so I inserted another finger and watched her squirm. "Oh, shit!"

If I didn't know any better, I would think her asshole was a virgin. I pulled my fingers out of her and my dick was begging to get in that ass, but she wasn't quite ready for that shit. I needed to get in something, though, so I stopped playing with her and sucked her clit with more force, causing her to nut instantly. She was already close to her release anyway. I knew it wouldn't take much more to get her there. "Fuck! Storm!"

She looked like a fish out of water the way her body was flopping on the sofa. I stared at her as I continued to give her my best, the inner workings of me. When she'd calmed down, I stood and said, "I'll be right back."

I had to get a condom. I wanted her so bad I didn't think to get that shit beforehand. When I got to the stairs, I moved as quickly as possible. Feeling her insides was next on my agenda and my ass got ahead of myself. Snatching a few condoms from the nightstand drawer, I quickly made my way back downstairs to dive into the shit that was my kryptonite and fuel all at the same time. She could bring me to my knees with that shit, but it also gave me the confidence to face whatever, just until it was time to feed that craving again.

When I got back downstairs, baby girl was sucking her own nipples, then flicked her tongue across them when she noticed me. I stroked my dick a couple of times, because the throbbing was starting to get painful. I had never wanted somebody so bad in my fucking life. Opening one of the condoms, I slid that shit on in record time and made my way to my big ol' freak. "Fuck! You so sexy, girl. Keep sucking them nipples."

I pushed those thick ass legs up to her head and drove my dick inside of her, coming to a head-on collision with that cervix. I closed my eyes and relished the feel of how her shit wrapped me up. Her scream when I entered her was one of passion that I couldn't ignore. Slowly pulling out, I looked down to see that she'd creamed all over my shit. That only broke the restraints off this dick, and he was in full control. I plowed into her repeatedly, grunting as I grabbed a handful of her hair. "Storm! Fuck! I'm cumming!"

And that she did... hard as hell. I slowed my assault but stroked her just as hard as I had been. Watching her pinch her nipples wasn't offering the help I needed to prolong my nut, so I pulled out of her and turned her on her side. Pushing forcefully inside of her again, I focused my attention on all that ass that was jiggling on my shit. Her sounds of passion were echoing throughout the room and puffing my chest up, knowing I was the cause of all what I was hearing. If I was more of a vocal person, she would know that she was doing just as much to me and how much of a struggle it was for me to make this shit last.

However, there wasn't much I could do to prolong it anymore. The tingling feeling swept over my body, and my muscles locked up like trailer brakes. That shit produced a growl out of me that made Aspen jump. "Fuck!"

My upper body collapsed on her as I panted. I felt so sensitive I couldn't move for shit. My dick was still inside of her and moving it was out of the question. Aspen didn't move a muscle, and she looked totally spent as well. This relationship was gon' be everything I knew it could be in the very beginning. Our chemistry was off the charts, and I couldn't help but to submit to that shit. I was just glad that she chose to submit to it, too.

---

"So, YOU TRYNA TELL ME WITHIN A MATTER OF TWO MONTHS, YOU done went from a man whore to a nigga all in love and shit?"

"I been tryna respect yo' ass by not calling you out of your name, but you making that shit hard to do. Even if I didn't have a girl now, it's my choice to not sleep wit'cho ass if I don't want to. I think it's just hurting your ego to know that you was just somebody to pass time with. But the truth is, you should have known that the first time we fucked. So, you was the last person I expected this shit from. I done had to block a couple, but I never thought you would have been the one tripping."

"You think that big bitch can give you everything I was giving you?"

Now I was steaming. She had me hotter than the flames of hell. My voice lowered, and it was filled with venom. "If you wasn't a woman, I'd come find you and beat the fuck out of your dumb ass. Bitches were what I was fucking around with before I found a real woman. You was the nastiest ho I ever dealt with. Let a nigga nut all in your face and anywhere I wanted and for what? What did you get out the deal? Gas money? Secondly, size ain't got shit to do with shit. She pleases me far better than anybody I ever had. That's the only shit that matters. Her heart is gold and she's the woman that can have it all, unlike yo' dick hopping ass."

I could hear her sniffling. So, I continued, "I know like hell the boss bitch ain't crying. Dry that shit the fuck up and move on. I wasn't the only nigga you was fucking. While I know its gon' be hella hard to replace a nigga like me, it's possible. Get on your prowl and leave me the fuck alone. Next time I won't be so nice about it."

I was sick of Nikki's ass. This would be the last time that I would address her ass. Why couldn't people just move the fuck on? Nikki and I were nothing more than fuck buddies. As I drove home, Aspen behind me in her Optima, I knew it was the perfect time to set Nikki straight, although, I knew I could've done that shit right in front of Aspen. I loved her level of confidence. She trusted me, and I promised myself that I would never betray her. Even when that nigga she was with tried to break her after she no longer wanted to be with him, she didn't let that shit keep her down.

We'd been at the hospital with Jasper and had gotten to meet his friend, Chasity. She'd eventually called hospitals until she found him. Jasper was grinning like he'd swallowed the canary the whole time she was there. Somehow, I'd missed seeing my parents at the hospital. I knew I needed to talk to them, especially my daddy. Our visit with Jasper was light, and he was feeling well. By the time we left, I was just ready to spend time with my baby.

We'd fucked literally all night. We saw the sunrise together and everything. Every area of my house had been christened, including the outside deck. We were supposed to be watching the sunrise together, but that shit didn't work out too well. I watched the sun rise on that ass, though. Afterward, Aspen cooked breakfast for us, and we finally brought our asses to bed.

When I'd awakened, I could hear her having a conversation on the phone and soon after, I realized it was her mama. I lay in the bed until I'd heard her end the call. She seemed a little off after that, so I wanted to remedy that. After her bath, I'd taken her shopping, and we'd gotten her a pair of boots. She was so damn happy for those boots she was practically dancing in the store. She wanted to embrace everything that I was interested in, and I appreciated that. So much so, until I bought her a Stetson, a blinged out belt, and a button-down shirt. If she let me, I was gonna spoil the hell out of her.

After spending time with Jasper, I had to get home, so my boy Zayson could get to the arena to practice. He and his team roping partner, Red, along with their friend Legend would be using my arena from time to time until Red's arena was done. When I told Aspen about that, she was talking about putting on her gear and going out there to watch. I had to laugh. I informed her that nobody would be dressed like that. Most times, they only wore that shit at the rodeos. After she poked her lip out, I had to promise to take her to a rodeo. I told her she could wear the hat, belt and boots for me later tonight, but she thought that shit was funny.

When we got to the house, I had her go in ahead of me, so she could park in the garage. As long as she was with me, we wouldn't be riding in that lil Optima. I was too tall for that shit. By the time we'd gotten in the house with our bags, I saw Zayson's truck at the intercom and another truck behind him. I opened the gate as baby girl went to the kitchen. "What are you doing, baby?"

"Well, I was gonna make some snacks for all of y'all to eat."

My eyebrows went up. *Damn.* She was gon' take care of me and the fellas like that? I didn't even know Legend like that. I knew Red, because he lived in Nome, too, and was a customer of mine, but I really didn't know him like that, either. "Them niggas don't need to be eating all my shit."

She looked at me seriously. I couldn't help but laugh. "It's cool, baby. If you wanna hook us up, that's cool. They probably won't want to eat until they're done, though."

The doorbell rang, and once I let the fellas in, I shook their hands, then introduced them to Aspen. Once the doorbell rang again, I was a little confused until Zayson said, "Oh, we invited the ladies, since we were gonna be out here. I hope that's okay."

"Fa show."

I opened the door for their wives and wife to be, a group of beautiful women. I took them inside to meet Aspen, and that was all she wrote. They were already vibing, so I headed outside with the fellas and looked forward to feeling a part of something for the first time in my life.

# CHAPTER 19

## ASPEN

Storm had literally begged me to stay with him longer, but I knew I had to get my shit together. My apartment would be ready in another week, so I agreed to come back and spend a few days with him once I got checked out. I'd been with him for four days, and it had been beyond amazing. To know and feel firsthand how tender he could be was overwhelming. Before that night in the club, I would have never imagined he could be so gentle. We fucked almost the entire time I was there, especially the last night. I was supposed to leave this morning to head back, but I didn't leave until two.

His friends were cool, too. It was crazy how much I had in common with their wives, especially Kortlynn. We'd all gotten along well, and Storm seemed to really be enjoying himself. He promised me that we would go to their next rodeo, and I couldn't wait to wear my new boots. I was so excited, I walked around his bedroom in them along with the cowboy hat for at least an hour. He thought that was the funniest thing. I grew up in the city, nowhere near anything country. So, it was exciting for me.

I'd even gone out with him to put out feed for the animals. I wanted to wear my boots then, but he said I needed work boots for

147

that. My boots were too dressy. Being with Storm was so exciting and I didn't want to leave, but I knew I had to. He really had me contemplating my living arrangement. The way he begged me to stay made it so difficult to back out of the driveway. That nigga had got on his knees and ate the entire fuck out of my pussy. I could barely walk after that shit. Those trembles had taken over my body and wouldn't go away.

As I lay across the hotel room's bed, I got a phone call. When I saw my mother's number, I decided to decline for now. I would call her later. She'd called me while I was at Storm's house and apologized for their behavior toward him. I couldn't take her apology seriously, though. Until they knew that Storm was loaded, they didn't want to hear anything about him. He owned a lil mechanic shop in a town that couldn't boast to have more than six hundred people in its population was their comeback. I believed she looked him up and saw the full-service center he owned.

I couldn't stand judgmental people, and I had no clue that my parents were that way until meeting Storm. My mama had explained that they wanted the best for me, but I also explained to her that Carlos definitely wasn't the one. She seemed to be accepting of that fact, but was still skeptical of Storm, making it seem like he was only pursuing me for what he could get from me. I wasn't a naïve little girl, but whatever. She offered for me to bring Storm to dinner after I'd gotten settled in my apartment, but that would totally be up to Storm.

Once I'd gotten some rest, I decided to start on Storm's writeup and had a great idea about writing our story. Just like he was falling for me, I was falling for him, too. I'd highlight his shop and the country side of him, but the way he pursued me and how I could no longer resist him would be the real story. Taking out my laptop, I began letting the words flow freely to describe the man that was slowly stealing my heart. He was passionate, genuine, loving, and rude as hell. He wasn't one that would let you get away with crossing him or beating him out of something. As I typed, my mind drifted back to when we first met. A slow smile crept up on my lips. I couldn't resist the urge after that.

I closed my laptop and began gathering my things to check out and head back to my man. Why did I want to pay to be alone when he literally begged me to stay? Just as I was about to head out to the car with my first round of things, my phone rang. I set the bags down and answered my father's call. Taking a deep breath, I answered, "Hello?"

"Hi, baby."

"Hi, Daddy."

"Listen. I'm sorry how things went down at the gala. There are some things that we need to talk to you about, but I would prefer it be face to face. Are you in town?"

"Well, I was just about to check out of the hotel and head back to Storm."

"Can you please meet us somewhere? Or can we meet you at your hotel before you leave? We were about to head back to Katy, but I feel like we need to make this right."

"Okay. I'm at Residence Inn on Westheimer. Room 236."

"Okay. We'll be there soon. Have you eaten?"

"No. But I'm not hungry. Thanks, Daddy."

"Okay. See you in a little bit."

I ended the call and worry flooded my being. What did they want to talk about that we couldn't talk about by phone? Looking at my phone in my hands, I decided to call the one person that could make me feel invincible and like nothing else in the world mattered but us. "Hello?"

I was silent for a while. His voice always did things to me, and I loved that shit. Listening to him breathe for a little longer, I closed my eyes, wishing I wouldn't have left him. "Hello?" he reiterated.

"Hey. Your voice just does things to me."

"Oh yeah? Things like what?"

"If I had time, I would tell you. But I needed you to soothe my racing heart. My parents are coming here to talk."

"I wish I could be there with you. You sound nervous. Listen to my voice and let that shit comfort your soul."

"Damn, baby."

"Yeah, and when they're done, I want you to come back. Call me crazy, but shit, I'm lonely as fuck in my own house."

I giggled a bit. "Baby, before they called, I'd packed up all my things and was about to head back."

"Shit, they should have called an hour later then."

"I know, right? I would've been almost there. I miss you already."

"I miss you, too. Had a nigga begging you to stay. When you get here, I need my man card back."

I laughed and he did, too. Man, he had me fiending to be in his arms, now. Each night I was there, if we weren't getting it in, he was holding me in his arms, making me feel safe. Whether he felt that way or not, he made me feel loved. His heart seemed to be so open to me, it was overwhelming. I nearly told him I loved him just because of how he'd made me feel. I was sitting here in the quietness, listening to him breathe. Closing my eyes, I took deep breaths, inhaling his positive energy, letting it rid the nervousness from my body. The knock on the door broke me from my meditation. "Baby, they're here."

"Okay. Call me when you're on your way home."

I smiled as I felt the butterflies flapping around. "Okay, baby. I... uh... I will."

I hurriedly ended the call as my heart raced. My thoughts had almost spilled out of my mouth. I almost told Storm that I loved him. *Did I love him?* I didn't think I loved him yet, but I cared for him deeply, that was for sure. Walking to the door, I looked through the peephole to be sure it was them, took a deep breath, and opened it. My parents both gave me soft smiles, then walked through the door after I stepped aside. They each kissed my cheek as they walked through to the sitting area.

They both sat on the sofa, and I sat in the chair across from them, waiting to see what warranted a face to face encounter. I was starting to fidget, because they looked almost as nervous as I did. "Well... umm... I guess I should get to it, so you can get on the road." Daddy glanced at my mama, then continued. "The reason we wanted you to be with Carlos was because we wanted their good stock. It would have been a business deal. However, when the two of you fell for one another, there was no need in saying anything. Had y'all not fell for one another, we would have arranged it."

I sat there for a moment, letting what he said sink in. Then a light bulb came on. "Carlos knew. He knew that it would benefit him to marry me. That's why he doesn't want to let go and tainted your view of Storm, thinking I would go along with what you guys wanted for me. Well, his plan backfired, because it made me want Storm even more. We're even closer than we were then."

"About Storm. You have to understand my anger. Imagine that your daughter brought a guy for you to meet in a public setting, and he punches a guy, knocking him out. Would you want your daughter with him?"

"Well, if I saw my daughter's ex at their table twice stirring up mess, I would have asked questions before calling her boyfriend a thug."

They both lowered their heads. I guess he thought I would see his point. "Aspen, we're about to have to file for bankruptcy. We just wanted you to be good. Taken care of."

"You wanted to make sure you guys were taken care of. I can take care of myself. How much will it take to get you out of debt?"

Truthfully, I would go broke for them. They'd always made sure I had the best of everything growing up. Dallas, too. Our parents spoiled the hell out of us. My daddy's pharmaceutical company was top shit back then. There was so much competition now, it was hard for them to keep up.

"Almost half a million, baby. But I can sell our home in Katy and move back to Houston in something smaller. That should profit us almost three hundred grand."

"While I'm not totally comfortable with your explanation for the way you treated Storm, I can help. Give me your account number, and I will wire you two hundred grand. I'm sure Dallas can help, too, but you guys have to say something."

"No. I can't let you do that," my daddy said.

"You don't have a choice. We bank at the same place. I can do it with or without your consent."

I'd saved quite a bit of money while Carlos and I were together. That was the only plus about him wanting to be the "man" and handle everything. My mama started crying, then stood and pulled me from my seat to hug me. "The gala was to help us as well. We advertised our services in hopes of getting more business, but after the Carlos and Storm incident, we lost some big donors. That's why we were so nasty and stressed, baby."

Now that made more sense. They were never usually that nasty. That was why I was so shocked by what had happened. "Now, that explanation I can believe. But there's someone else you owe an apology to. Storm is the most amazing man I've ever met."

"You look to be happy, Aspen," my mama said.

"I'm extremely happy. Now if you two don't mind, could you help me bring all this to my car?"

"Of course, baby."

That talk went a lot better than I thought it would, and I was so grateful to be getting back to Storm. I knew once I was there, though, there was no way he was going to let me leave again, and I was okay with that.

# CHAPTER 20

## STORM

"Good morning, baby."

Aspen turned over in the bed, rolling herself up in the covers. She'd gotten in late last night, and I was sure to welcome her back home. I had to go to the shop this morning. Although we were up until two this morning, I'd gotten some sleep while she was in Houston before she came back. I chuckled and kissed her cheek, then headed to the shop.

I also knew I had to talk to my parents. I'd been putting off the inevitable long enough. The sheriff department had called me and said that Marcus had made bail. Marcus was the secret son of my daddy. I knew that could only mean one thing. My dad had bailed him out. When I got to work, I got a couple of hellos as I headed to my office. I wasn't getting a good vibe, though. Some shit seemed off. Just as I thought that, the supervisor knocked on my door. "Hello, Mr. Henderson. Can I speak to you for a moment?"

I exhaled loudly. "Yeah."

"Several people said they'd seen Curtis stealing tires over the weekend. So, I went through the surveillance videos and sure enough, he was rolling them out of here Saturday and Sunday night."

"I'm gon' fuck his ass up. What time he come to work?"

"Two o'clock."

"How did he get a key? That muthafucka shouldn't have a key."

"I don't know, sir."

"Do we have any customers besides Mr. Charlie?"

"No, sir."

"Good. Lock the fucking doors."

I stood from my chair that I'd just sat in and pushed it against the wall. Muthafuckas were always trying to test me. I went to the front and said, "I'm sorry, Mr. Charlie, forgive me for what you about to hear." I paused for a second, then said, "All y'all mutha- fuckas come to my office. Gerald, go get them from outside."

I went back to the office with a trail of employees behind me. Once the others had made it inside, I looked from face to face. "So, I hear Curtis is stealing from me. This meeting about to be short as hell. I catch a muthafucka stealing from me, I'm gon' fuck you up before the police can. So, I would heed my warning. If you have questions, talk to your supervisor. If that don't help, talk to the store manager. I'm yo' last resort. But if one of y'all stealing, I'm gon' be your first problem. Don't let the last name fool you. Get the fuck outta here."

I looked at the supervisor and said, "I'll be right back."

I knew where Curtis lived, and when I hopped those railroad tracks, he was gon' feel my fury. I hopped in my pickup and just as I was about to peel out, my cell phone rang. "Hello?"

"Good morning, baby. I'm sorry. I'm drained."

"It's okay. Why you up?"

"I don't know. My eyes just popped open. You okay? You sound pissed."

"Found out one of my employees is stealing from me, and when I find out who gave him a key and the alarm code, I'm gon' fuck them up, too."

"Baby, come home first. Pleeeaaaasssse?"

154

I couldn't help but chuckle. "Let me go handle this business first."

"Babyyyy… but I'm horny as fuck."

"Aspen… come on, na. You know I can't resist yo' sexy ass. I need to go put this nigga on notice."

"Can you put him on notice after?"

"Fuck! A'ight! I can't put him on notice with a hard dick. He better thank yo' ass, too."

I ended the call and shook my head slowly, then made my way to Aspen.

---

"Seven! I'm surprised to see you here!"

"Hey, Ma. What y'all up to?"

"Umm… not too much. What about you?"

She seemed so damn nervous. I already knew they bailed that nigga out of jail, but I was willing to bet he was here. That was why her ass was so nervous. "Not too much. My baby back."

"So, y'all official now?"

"Yep. For once, I want a woman around me all the time."

"That's good, baby. I'm happy for you, Seven. You've come a long way."

"Well, it was worth the wait. Where's Daddy?"

"He… uh… He's in the den."

"What'chu all nervous and shit for?"

"Why you think I'm nervous?"

"And now you stalling. Mama, I know you. So, quit playing. I already know y'all bailed him out. Since I was the point of contact for the police, they let me know when he made bail."

Mama looked like she wanted to throw up. She walked toward the back, and I followed her. After I'd fucked the shit out of Aspen's ass, she went back to sleep. I knew she was trying to calm me down, and it was a good thing she did. I probably would have ended up in jail today. I was gon' beat the fuck out of Curtis ass with my .38.

Instead, I went to his crib and found my shit, then I fired his ass and took the key from him. He claimed he'd gotten it from the night supervisor. That muthafucka was next on my hitlist as soon as I left here. Curtis's ass had better been glad I'd recovered my shit or I would have pressed charges on his ass. I was still pissed when I got there, but I wasn't feeling hostile, thanks to Aspen.

As I continued to follow Mama, sure enough, Daddy was sitting there talking to Marcus. I could feel the scowl taking over my facial expression. Daddy and Marcus stood to their feet quickly. Marcus said, "I'm gonna go."

"Naw. Stay."

He looked between my dad and me, trying to decide what he should do, I supposed. I sat down to make that decision a little easier on him. He and Dad sat hesitantly, their eyes staying on me. Shit, they were making me feel like I was a damn monster or some shit, but I was glad to know that they feared a nigga. People around town that knew me also knew it wasn't good if you were on my bad side.

"Look. I done had some time to calm down about this. Ain't shit I can do but move on from it. Am I gon' be walking around announcing that I have a lil brother? Hell, naw. But the animosity is gone. Daddy, if Mama can forgive you for your betrayal, and Marcus can forgive you for neglecting him, then I can forgive you for lying to us."

"Storm, I didn't lie."

"In my book, a secret kept away from the people you love is your neglect to tell the truth. A lie."

He nodded his head. "I'm sorry, son. I spoke to your siblings a couple of days ago, but I wanted to give you time to cool off. You're a lot like me. If you hadn't come here by tomorrow, I was going to go to you. I love you, Storm, and it was never my intent to hurt you or any of your brothers and sisters. It was a poor choice that I made, but something innocent came out it: Marcus. I made him suffer for my poor judgment."

I nodded my head, but I didn't miss the slight frown on Marcus's face. Maybe their talk wasn't going as well as I thought it was. "It bothered me so much, because everything I do, I patterned after you. As a kid, I always wanted to be like you. I even felt that way as a man. Putting you on a pedestal and deeming you perfect, only set myself up for disappointment. You're human and bound to mess up. I'm sorry for my disrespect, and you're still a good man that I will continue to look up to. I hate it had to come to all this, but I'm glad that everything is out in the open now, so everybody involved can heal from this, especially you, Marcus."

My dad stood from his seat and hugged me. He patted my back a couple of times, then released me. I looked over at Marcus and extended my hand. He shook it, then nodded at me. "A'ight, well I gotta go fire somebody, then spend time with my baby."

"Fire somebody?" my daddy asked.

"Yeah. Curtis was stealing tires from the shop over the weekend. I fired him, but I have to fire the supervisor that gave him the key. Thanks to Aspen, I didn't go to jail for assaulting him on his property today."

My dad shook his head slowly. "So, you and Aspen official?"

"Yeah. So, I guess I can thank you for this lil scandal you had going on. I wouldn't have met her if Marcus wouldn't have been trying to ruin you."

They both chuckled a bit. "Well, congratulations. I liked her for you the moment I met her."

"Thanks. Well, I'm out. Hopefully, I don't have to beat nobody ass."

I stood and shook their hands as I left. Trying to get in the frame of mind to go off on the bum ass supervisor at my job, I put a frown on my face before I even left out of the house. My mama stopped me before I could leave. "Is everything okay?"

"Yeah, Ma. Everything's cool. I gotta go to the shop and set some shit straight."

"Okay. Well, I know you aren't about to leave without telling me bye."

"Sorry. I do need to apologize to you to for my behavior at the hospital. I know you were embarrassed."

"A little, but that's our fault for spoiling your ass, always letting you have your way."

I twisted my lips to the side as she laughed, then kissed her cheek and headed out. Aspen and I would come back later. I left out and went to the shop. As soon as I got there, my anger kicked up a notch. I got out of the truck and went inside, looking for Jackson's ass. After I didn't see him up front or outside, I asked one of the clerks, "Where Jackson?"

"He went to the back."

I walked down the hallway to the only office they had access to when I wasn't here. This muthafucka was sitting down with his feet up on the got damn desk. When he saw me, he hurriedly put them on the floor, but it was too late. "What the fuck you in here doing? I ain't hire yo' ass to be chilling wit'cho fucking feet on the desk."

"I know. I'm sorry, Storm."

"Man, don't call me Storm. I'm Mr. Henderson to yo' ass. We ain't friends. Why Curtis got a key to my damn store?"

"I needed to leave early Friday night, and I asked him to lock up for me."

"You should have called me or the store manager."

"I apologize. I planned to get the key back from him today, but he didn't show up to work."

"That's because I fired his ass for stealing, and you finna be in the unemployment line with his ass. Get yo' shit and get the fuck outta here."

"Please, Mr. Henderson. I need my job."

"You should've thought about that shit Friday."

I walked out and went to the front and sat. I wanted to watch them run the store, and I wanted to stay until Jackson brought his ass out of that office. The longer I sat there, the more I felt like he set that whole shit up. Curtis wasn't that damn smart, and it showed by the camera footage. Ain't no way he would've decided, upon himself, to steal from me. The longer he took to come from back there, the hotter I got.

Standing from my seat, I went back there to see this nigga on the phone. "Nigga, what you doing? When I said get yo' shit and get the fuck out of here, that meant now!"

I snatched the phone from him and grabbed him by the shirt, practically dragging him out the room while everyone watched. He must have wanted to be embarrassed with the way he was fucking with me. When I got to the door, I almost threw his ass through it. "Mr. Henderson, I didn't get all my things."

"I'll mail that shit to you. You had plenty of time to get yo' shit. You got five fucking minutes to leave or you gon' have to deal with the nigga in me that you ain't met yet. So, I suggest you get the fuck on, ASAP, and don't bring yo' ass back over here. If I find proof you had anything to do with Curtis stealing merchandise, I'm pressing charges on yo' ass. I feel like you do, but I can't prove that shit right now."

His shoulders slumped, then he walked his pitiful ass to his car. This shit really pissed me off, because now I had to stay here the rest of the day. I'd forgotten that the fucking store manager would be out of town until the weekend. Once he drove off, I went to my office and called Aspen. "Hello?"

"Baby, I have to stay at the shop until six. I had to fire the supervisor and the store manager is out of town."

"Okay, baby. Handle your business. I'll have a surprise waiting for you when you get home."

"If it involves yo' ass butt naked, then I can't wait."

"That, plus some."

"Aww shit. I can't wait. I can still taste you on my lips and smell you in my beard. I feel like a damn hound dog, 'cause I'm on yo' scent."

She laughed loudly, but I was serious as hell. I had to stay in my office for a minute after talking to Aspen to calm my dick down. It was hard to believe that all this started from a blown tire. I wanted her then, but it was strictly lust. Her refusal of me, even at my most persuasive time, made me look at her for who she was and not just that sex appeal she was slanging.

Tonight was going to be special, in more ways than one.

# CHAPTER 21
## ASPEN

I couldn't wait for Storm to get home. I'd cooked his favorite: ox tails, black-eyed peas with rice, cabbage, and candied yams. Although I'd spent a fortune at the grocery store in Sour Lake, it was worth it for Storm. I could've gotten this for half the price in Houston. It was like they charged people for living in a rural area with these prices.

Once I'd cooked his meal, I cleaned up a bit just to give myself something to do. I put on some extremely short shorts and a tank top that my titties would easily spill out of, after soaking in the tub, preparing my body for tonight's festivities.

When I heard Storm in the driveway, I slipped on my heels and prepared to meet him at the door. He'd had a rough day already, so I was praying that the second half of his day was a little easier. When I heard his keys, I walked closer to the door and struck a pose. I giggled inside, because I felt a little silly doing this. But the way he made me feel pulled even more confidence out of me and made me feel like the most desired woman in the world. I brought my hand up to my head and grabbed my hair.

Focusing my eyes on the door when it opened, I felt a tinge of nervousness course through me. Storm looked pissed as he closed the door, but the way all that shit left his face when he saw me was priceless. He tucked his bottom lip in his mouth and scanned my body from head to toe. "Hey, baby. How was the rest of your day?"

"Shit, I don't even remember, now," he said as he made his way to me, holding his dick through his pants. "Fuck, Aspen. You sexy as hell."

I smiled at him, then put my arms around his neck when he'd made it to me. "You sexy as hell, too. I can't wait to see what category you gon' unleash on me tonight."

"Category? Naw. This shit is about to be the deadliest tornado you ever seen."

He gripped my ass tightly, causing me to flinch, then lowered his mouth to my neck. "Storm, we can't start yet. I cooked for you, baby."

"But I got my dinner right here," he mumbled against my neck.

"So, you don't want ox tails, yams, cabbage, and black-eyed peas?"

His head snapped up before I could even finish. I laughed as he stared at me with a serious look on his face and his mouth slightly opened. "You wouldn't fuck with me like that, would you? You really cooked all that?"

"Hell, yeah. Go take a shower while I prepare your plate."

Storm stood there for a moment, then smiled at me. "Man, you the shit, babe. I'll be right back."

He kissed my lips, then took off for the stairs. Storm made me feel like a school-aged girl the way he had me in here giggling all the damn time. I didn't think I would be able to move on as quickly as I did with him, but it felt so natural. There wasn't a moment where I felt I was rushed, and I could attribute that to the fact that I hadn't loved Carlos for a long time.

It was like we were living as roommates with benefits, aside from the fact that I wasn't paying for shit. The whole situation with him made me feel a way. I believed that had I not met Storm, I would have dwelled on it a little more. He was pretty much upset that the business deal had fallen through. His aggressiveness had nothing to do with me. Storm was a welcomed distraction from all that bullshit. He helped me be able to handle that shit internally and move the hell on.

I made our plates and set them on the dining table, then brought our tea. I'd also brought me a glass of wine and him a Heineken as well. For dessert, I'd made a strawberry cake, which was also one of his favorites. I could hear him moving around upstairs, so he was done with his shower. I turned on some music by a young lady named Brayla, one of my cousin's students that she'd turned me on to and waited for him to come down the stairs.

When he joined me in the dining area, his eyes widened. "Baby, this look good. Thank you."

"You're welcome. Sit."

I didn't have to tell him twice. He immediately sat and I sat next to him. We held hands as he said the blessing, then got to it. Storm brought the first forkful of peas and rice to his mouth and moaned. I smiled big, knowing that he was pleased. After swallowing, he said, "Damn, baby. This is good."

"Thank you."

We sat there eating, occasionally feeding one another until we were done. The silence between us was overwhelming, because you could cut the sexual tension right along with the strawberry cake. I could tell Storm had lots of illicit shit on his mind, and I was here for every minute of it. As I put his cake in front of him, he pulled me to him and lifted my shirt. His lips went across my stomach, sending chills up my spine.

Taking the fork, he cut into his piece of cake and brought it to my mouth. I sensually took it from the fork as I stared into his eyes. This nigga stood from his chair and pushed everything, except the cake, off the table. He set me there and pulled my shirt off. "You gon' break this table."

"Fuck this table."

He spread some of the icing across my nipples, then sucked them like it was the best thing he'd ever tasted. I rested my hands at the back of his head, gently stroking the waves in his hair, and dropped my head back. "Seven… shit."

He lay me back on the table, and I got a little uncomfortable. Falling was the last thing I wanted to do. This damn table may not be strong enough to hold my weight, but Storm didn't seem to be the least bit bothered. "Chill out, girl. I got'chu."

He pulled my shorts off and spread my legs, then dropped his sweats. He must've put a condom in his pocket after his shower, because he strapped up and entered me like he had a fire to put out. Little did he know, this fire would always be blazing for him. "Ahh, fuck, Aspen. Shit, girl. Your pussy is so fucking good."

I stared at him, not knowing what to say. Storm never really talked during sex. He made grunting noises and occasionally cursed, but that was the extent of it. There were never complete sentences, besides the first time. My orgasm was coming to greet me already, because his words had taken me there. "Stooorm."

"Naw. Don't cum yet. I got some shit I need to say first."

My eyes widened. All this talking was making me wanna cum even quicker, and he wanted me to hold the shit in? "Ahhh, baby. I'm trying to hold it in."

He stroked me slowly as his skin reddened. "Aspen, I don't know what you've done to me, but you've changed me, for real. I've never felt so fucking happy in all my life."

My body was trembling, trying to release the orgasm he asked me to hold. Leaning over me, he continued to stroke me, taking my body to places I wasn't going to return from until I could release. He kissed my lips passionately as my clit felt like it was about to explode. When he pulled away from me, he said, "Open your eyes, girl."

This was pure torture. He was making love to me, wanting me to hold my orgasm, and now, he wanted me to look at him. I slowly opened my eyes, and the passion I saw in his was overwhelming. "I guess what I'm trying to tell you is that I love you, baby."

That shit did it. I came all over him. I'd never been a crier, especially not during sex, but the tears sprang from my eyes as I wrapped my arms around his neck. "Shit! I love you, too, Storm."

He continued making love to me on that table and staring into my eyes. Once he came, we continued the staring game until he said, "Let's go upstairs now. I'm about to fuck the shit out of you."

---

As we knocked on my parents' front door, Storm said, "I feel like I'm about to be ambushed."

I chuckled. "Storm, it's gon' be cool. I promise."

It had been a week, and Storm had gone back and forth in his mind on whether he was going to come or not. Thoughts of their last exchange made him want to say fuck it all, but he'd finally decided to come and let me know that he was definitely doing this for me. In return, I promised him that we wouldn't stay longer than a couple of hours, unless he wanted to. Seeing the for-sale sign in the yard had caught me off guard, so I was almost as uneasy as he was. When my mom opened the door, she smiled and stepped aside to let us in. "Hi, Aspen. Hello, Storm."

I kissed her cheek, then she nodded at Storm and led us to their dining area where Daddy was already seated. When we entered, he stood from his seat to greet us. After kissing my cheek, he extended his hand to Storm. Hesitantly, he shook it. I wanted to laugh, because I could see the wheels turning in his head. He was expecting the worst and had built a damn steel wall around himself. We were seated at the table, and Mama went to the kitchen to bring the food to the table. I wanted to help her, but I didn't want to leave Storm alone with Daddy until all was well.

It was a simple meal of baked fish, salad, and mixed vegetables. I knew we would be stopping for more to eat on our way back to Nome. I'd been in Nome the entire week, and Storm told me that I wouldn't be going anywhere else. I had to let my apartment go because I was going to end up paying for something he wasn't going to even allow me to move into.

Expressing my love for him and his for me had taken the both of us on an emotional ride that night. The next day, neither of us could move. We were so sore from the lovemaking we'd done, we had to soak in his tub. He didn't even allow me to that alone. I'd laid against his chest in the huge air tub and let him hold me.

The whole moment was so intimate I knew that I'd never leave to move anywhere else. Seven Storm Henderson was the man I loved, and I could only pray that it passed the test of time. I had strong faith that it would. After Daddy said grace, we began eating. It was so quiet, you could hear a pin drop, or as Storm once said, you could hear a rat piss on cotton. His ass was so damn country, it was crazy.

Finally, Daddy broke the silence. "Storm, I can tell you're uneasy. So, instead of waiting until after dinner, I'll say it now. We want to apologize for our behavior the night of the gala, especially my behavior. The things I said were cruel, misdirected, and ignorant."

Storm shifted in his seat, but he remained quiet. "My daughter seems to be so happy, and there is nothing that we want more. If you make her that happy, then you're great in our book. Again, we apologize for our actions and behavior."

Storm glanced at me, then turned back to them as they awaited his response. "We're good."

I smiled big as I nudged him. He smiled back at me, and I could immediately feel him relax. "So, Storm, what are some things you like to do? I was thinking we could take time to get to know one another. I don't mind getting dirty, because Aspen said you love animals."

Storm chuckled as I immediately thought about the time I asked him that question. That nigga told me he liked to fuck, so I was waiting to see what he would say to my daddy. "Well, not just any animals, but I love farm animals. I would also like to learn how to play golf."

I leaned dramatically in my chair, looking at Storm in surprise. That nigga had never told me he wanted to learn to play golf. He never even told me he was interested in the sport. The table laughed, and Storm relaxed even more. He pulled me to him and kissed me. "Yo' man interested in other things, girl. Not just country stuff."

It was funny not hearing a curse word in that statement, but I knew he was being respectful to my parents. As we ate, they conversed like there was never a rift between them, and I couldn't be more excited about their budding friendship. I was so comfortable with it that I helped my mama clean up. When we got to the kitchen, she smiled at me. "I'm so happy for you, baby. Storm is kind of hot."

My eyebrows went up. "Mom!"

"What? He is!"

I laughed. She'd never been so open with me about a boyfriend of mine. "I know! Mom, last week, he told me for the first time that he loved me. It was so tender, it made me cry."

"Wow, baby. That's beautiful. Like your dad said, as long as he makes you happy, then we're happy. There's no doubt in my mind that he can protect you. He knocked the hell out of Carlos."

I let my head drop as I laughed. I liked the personality Storm had brought out of them. They were more fun than I thought, and my dad saying that he would get dirty took the cake, too. His whole aura made us all better. Even with his tough demeanor, he was sweet as cotton candy beneath it all. I smiled as I put dishes in the dishwasher, thanking God for putting me in the eye of the Storm.

# EPILOGUE

## STORM

### SIX MONTHS LATER...

"Mr. St. Andrews, just loosen up. He's gentle, but he can sense fear."

Aspen's parents had come to Nome to visit, and today was day three of their stay. Her dad decided that he wanted to try to ride a horse. I chuckled at the expression on his face once he'd gotten up there, and my dad had to nudge me. Aspen's dad was so damn city. He didn't know shit about the country besides the rodeos, and he really didn't know shit about that. I mounted my horse, my dad and Jasper doing the same, and I directed Mr. St. Andrews on what to do next.

As we rode, and he'd gotten more comfortable, I let my mind drift to how great things had been. My business was still thriving, the cattle farms were doing better than ever, and my love life with Aspen was getting better every day. When I thought it couldn't get any better, she'd shown me something that disputed that. The past six months had been unbelievable. She made a nigga feel like a king. I mean I was a self-pronounced king, but to have someone who genuinely made me feel like one was a totally different thing.

169

Aspen was my rock, and I loved every minute of being able to depend on someone else for happiness. While I knew that happiness was within and that I shouldn't base it on another person or what they did, it was hard not to. Without her, I knew I wouldn't even be the same person that I was today. I'd been spending more time with Marcus since the charges were dropped against him. It turned out that the guy that was with him was the one taking out everybody else's cattle. Marcus had solicited his help to get back at our daddy.

He was now working at my shop and daddy was grooming him to own his own business as well. Things seemed like they couldn't get any better on that front, either. For once in my life, it seemed like everything was perfect. I almost didn't think Aspen would actually move in with me. While I knew I kind of forced her hand, she could've gotten angry and said, *fuck you,* but she trusted that I was making the right decision for the both of us. Her being with me forever was definitely the right decision.

After our horse ride, Mr. St. Andrews had a look of excitement on his face. I chuckled, because I'd never seen that much excitement in a man over the age of fifty. "Storm, I can tell you now, me and Celeste will be spending a lot of time out this way. I really enjoyed this."

"I'm glad you did."

He and my dad went off to the deck at the back of the house to talk and smoke cigars while I went inside to check on my baby. When I walked in, the women were all running around, scaring the shit out of me. "What's going on?"

"Seven, get the hell out of here! I'll come get you when we're ready."

I frowned at my mama, trying to figure out what the hell she was talking about. *How the hell she was gon' put me outta my own damn house?* Before I could say anything, Jasper's girlfriend, Chasity, said, "Please, Storm. It's important that you do what your mama said. Aspen's gonna be upset if you don't."

My frown only deepened, but just the thought of Aspen being

angry was enough to make me walk the fuck outta my own house without knowing shit about what I just saw.

## ASPEN

*Pregnant.* I stared at that test for minutes, totally in shock. I loved Storm, but I didn't know how he would take this information. We'd talked about having kids one day, but we never specified how soon we wanted that to happen. We'd been so busy getting comfortable in our relationship, learning more and more about each other as the days passed, we hadn't made time to seriously discuss it.

Things had been so perfect. So, I was hoping that this only made them better. Living here with Storm had been the best decision he'd ever made me make. Chuckling at the thought, I realized he really didn't give me much of a choice. When I'd gotten our story published, it was like his heart opened even more. I didn't think it could open up to me any more than it already was, but the way I described him as the man that I loved, caused him to become even more tender with me. We haven't had a serious argument, yet, and when we did disagree, we quickly cleared that shit up. I was grateful that he was different with me.

With everyone else, Storm was stubborn, rude, a jackass, and could stew in his anger for days… pretty much the same way he was with me when we first met. Over time, the tenderness he exuded when it came to me left me speechless. At thirty-one years old, I'd never experienced a love so deep. As I stood in the bathroom, I was trying to figure out how I would reveal this to him. My mom and his mom, along with Jasper's girlfriend, were keeping watch to make sure he didn't come in the house until I was ready to tell him.

I'd been feeling bloated all week, so I'd gone to the store and bought a test. My cycle was late, so I suspected it. When I took the test while they were out riding horses, I screamed when I saw the results. My mama and Mrs. Henderson had come running to the bathroom to see what was going on. The way my mama hugged me and cradled me let me know how happy she was. She was feeling as sensitive about this as I was. However, the way Mrs. Henderson had danced around the house had made us laugh and break out of that sensitivity we were feeling.

I finally came out of the bathroom as they all stared at me with huge smiles on their faces. I wiped the lone tear that fell from my eye, and my mama said, "My baby's gonna have a baby."

That caused more tears to fall down my cheeks as well as hers. They all hugged me tightly in a group hug as Storm burst through the door. "Look! I don't know what the hell going on, but somebody gon' tell me something. I been outside for ten minutes, pacing and…"

He stopped mid-sentence when he looked at the tears on my face. Storm made his way to me so quickly it was like he was a damned tornado. The ladies all moved out the way as I said, "Tell everyone else to come inside."

"Baby, what's wrong? Is it something I did? Whatever it is, I'm sorry. Seeing you cry is breaking me, girl."

I lifted my hands to his face and kissed him to settle him down. He was a nervous wreck. I could hear Jasper say, "Aww hell naw. I know y'all didn't call us in here to see them sucking each other face off. I don't wanna see that shhh… stuff."

Everyone laughed as he filtered himself. When I broke our kiss, Storm was staring at me seriously, not even a smirk on his lips. "Baby, I have an announcement to make."

That was when the smirk appeared. His attentive ass probably already knew. Just as I suspected, he picked me up and spun me around as I screamed, and the women laughed. Jasper had a frown on his face and in that instance, he and Storm looked even more alike. "Damn, girl. For real?"

I nodded my head and he kissed me passionately in front of everybody. When he pulled away, he said, "A'ight. Y'all gotta go find y'all something else to do. We need a couple of hours."

"So, what was the announcement?" Storm's dad asked with a confused look on his face that mirrored my dad and Jasper's.

We all laughed, and when I composed myself, I said, "I'm pregnant."

## The End

If you did not read the author's note at the beginning, please go back and do so before leaving a review. ☺

# FROM THE AUTHOR...

I hope you enjoyed this country love story! Storm was something else... chiiiile! He was bullying me at times. But I love how Aspen was able to calm his ass down. There was so much to unpack though, and this is only the beginning.

As always, I gave it my all. Whether you liked it or not, please take the time to leave a review on Amazon and/or Goodreads.

There's also an amazing playlist on Apple Music and Spotify for this book, under the same title that includes some great R&B, rap, and even zydeco tracks to tickle your fancy.

Please keep up with me on Facebook, Instagram, and TikTok (@authormonicawalters), Twitter (@monlwalters), and Clubhouse (@monicawalters). You can also visit my Amazon author page at www.amazon.com/author/monica.walters to view my releases.

Please subscribe to my webpage for updates and sneak peeks of upcoming releases! https://authormonicawalters.com.

For live discussions, giveaways, and inside information on upcoming releases, join my Facebook group, Monica's Romantic Sweet Spot at https://bit.ly/2P2l06X.

## FROM THE AUTHOR...

# OTHER TITLES BY MONICA WALTERS

Love Like a Nightmare

Forbidden Fruit (An Erotic Novella)

Say He's the One

Only If You Let Me

On My Way to You (An Urban Romance)

8 Seconds to Love

Breaking Barriers to Your Heart

Any and Everything for Love

Savage Heart (A Crossover Novel with Shawty You for Me by T Key)

I'm In Love with a Savage (A Crossover Novel with Trade It All by T Key)

Don't Tell Me No (An Erotic Novella)

To Say, I Love You: A Short Story Anthology with the Authors of BLP

Behind Closed Doors Series

Be Careful What You Wish For

You Just Might Get It

Show Me You Still Want It

Sweet Series

Bitter Sweet

Sweet and Sour

Sweeter Than Before

Sweet Revenge

Sweet Surrender

Sweet Temptation

Sweet Misery

Sweet Exhale

## Motives and Betrayal Series

Ulterior Motives

Ultimate Betrayal

Ultimatum: #lovemeorleaveme, Part 1

Ultimatum: #lovemeorleaveme, Part 2

## Written Between the Pages Series

The Devil Goes to Church Too

The Book of Noah (A Crossover Novel with The Flow of Jah's Heart by T Key)

The Revelations of Ryan, Jr. (A Crossover Novel with All That Jazz by T Key)

Made in the USA
Coppell, TX
28 January 2025

45111218R00111